HALL

VOLUMES 1-3

The Case of the
Snow White Lady

Sherlock Holmes
and the Deathly Fog

The Case of the
Curious Cabinet

LIZ HEDGECOCK

WHITE
RHINO
BOOKS

ISBN-13: 978-1726831130

The Case of the Snow White Lady

I

Despite the weak autumn sunlight, there was a distinct nip in the air as I crossed Regent's Park. The cold wind found its way through my scarf, down my shirt-collar, and even up my trouser-legs, and I quickened my pace until I almost panted as I reached the steps of 221B Baker Street.

Mrs Hudson opened the door herself, and her face was wreathed in smiles at the sight of me. 'I'm so glad it's you, Dr Watson. Perhaps you can stir Mr Holmes to action.'

'Another one of his gloomy fits?' I asked, hanging up my hat and shrugging off my ulster.

'I'm afraid so, doctor. He needs a good case.'

'Well, as it happens, I may have the remedy right here.' I tapped my pocket and mounted the stairs, smiling to myself at Mrs Hudson's solicitude.

I found Sherlock Holmes lying on the sofa, his violin in his lap and his bow arm dangling. 'Things must be bad if you can't even be bothered to make a noise.' I took a fingerful of tobacco from the Persian slipper and sank into the chair opposite.

'What's the point?' said Holmes. 'What's the point of anything?'

'To rid the streets of crime,' I said, somewhat sententiously, as I filled my pipe.

'Ha!' snorted Holmes. 'I catch one criminal, and another fills his place. So dull. And all the same; there's no variety.'

'No one said it was fun, Holmes.'

'I just want a nice easy life. What's wrong with that?'

It was my turn to snort. 'Holmes, that is the last thing you want and you know it. Nothing would buck you up more than a juicy case. And I' — I pulled an envelope from my pocket — 'have just the thing.'

Holmes's drooping eyelids snapped open. 'What is it? Give it to me.'

'I shall read it to you.' I drew the letter from the

envelope, perhaps a little more slowly than I needed to.

'Come on, man!' Holmes's eyes glittered, and his long fingers twitched.

I unfolded the sheets and cleared my throat. 'The letter is from an old school friend of mine. We had lost touch, but — as your biographer I also have a certain notoriety.'

'Out with it!' cried Holmes.

I smiled to myself, and read aloud:

Dear Watson,

Forgive me renewing our acquaintance in this way, with a plea for assistance. I am at my wits' end. I thought I had been tried enough, but no —

Excuse my disjointed scribbles, but I am beside myself. My only daughter died last month. She was ill for some time, and we knew the end must come soon. But it is not the end. She has been sighted walking abroad in the evenings — on the moor, in the village, in the churchyard! You will say this is fancy and superstition, a ghost, but it is worse than that. Witnesses say she has blood on her lips, and they have seen her pick up dogs and cats, bite them, and suck their blood. The villagers talk of the Snow-White Lady, and I fear my daughter has become — I can scarcely bring myself to write

3

it — a vampire!

Watson, I can trust you. Please come down to Dartmoor and examine my daughter's body, so that I can set my mind at rest. And your friend, the celebrated Mr Holmes, if he cares to look into this... I am a rational man, not a fool, but the evidence is such to make me doubt every belief that I hold dear. Please wire me by return, and say you will come.

Yours in desperation,
William Holcombe, Esq.

I looked over the top of the letter, expecting to see Holmes's eyes fixed on me, but he had vanished with his usual catlike stealth. From the bedroom I heard muffled muttering.

'Are you all right, Holmes?' I called.

Sherlock Holmes appeared in the doorway, a shirt in one hand and two neckties in the other. 'Am I all right?' He beamed. 'A death, a moor, a churchyard, and a vampire? Never better, Watson, never better!' His eyes narrowed. 'You've got a change of clothes in that bag, haven't you?'

I nodded.

'Then let us be off! Mrs Hudson, we have a case!' And the door of 221B banged behind us.

II

'Tell me something of your friend,' Holmes said, as the train rattled through the darkening countryside.

'There isn't much to tell,' I said. 'Well, there may be, but I do not know it. Bill Holcombe left school quite abruptly when I was fourteen. A distant relative died unexpectedly, and Holcombe's father inherited Mickleton Hall, in Devon. We said we would write to each other, but —' I spread my palms. 'Out of sight, out of mind, I suppose.'

'Quite so.' Holmes rubbed his hands. 'An ancestral hall, too? Oh, if I only had my index to hand!'

'You will see it soon enough,' I said. 'I wired Holcombe to say we were coming down tonight. From the tone of his letter, I imagine someone will meet us at the station.'

'But how will we find them?' frowned Holmes.

I glanced at the keen profile reflected in the train window, framed with a deerstalker and caped overcoat, as was Holmes's wont for rural cases. 'I do not think we need to worry ourselves on that score.'

My intuition proved right. We had barely stepped from the train at Exeter St Davids when a strapping, tweed-suited man hurried towards us. 'Mr Holmes, sir? I am Mr Week, Mr Holcombe's land agent.' Never was a man less aptly named, I reflected as Week wrung first Holmes's, and then my hand. 'Mr Holcombe would have come himself, but — he does not like to be out after dark.' A shadow passed over his broad, ruddy face.

'I quite understand, Mr Week. I am sorry we have kept you waiting so long. I take it your gig is securely tethered now, and your horse calm.'

Mr Week first looked suspicious, then his chest heaved in a hearty laugh. 'You are every bit as good as they say, Mr Holmes.' He leaned in, conspiratorially. 'Go on, tell me how you did it.'

'I can tell you, Mr Week, but you will think it nothing more than a children's conjuring trick.' Holmes sighed. 'Very well. The mud splashes on your trousers indicate that you drove yourself, and their pattern — no higher than your calf — suggests a gig, as it has a high driver's seat.' Holmes opened his hand. 'Your handshake has left small traces of newsprint, yet you were not reading a paper when the train came in, suggesting you have finished and disposed of it while you waited. Finally, the cleft of your thumb shows a fresh red mark, similar to a rope burn. I conjectured that your horse had startled and required a firm hand to restrain it.'

Mr Week grinned. 'It does seem simple when you explain it.'

'Sometimes the simplest things seem most complicated,' said Holmes. 'I take it the servants do not know of my engagement, hence your journey.'

'The less they know, the less gossip they can spread,' said Mr Week. 'Let's get going. The last part of the journey is not best undertaken in pitch dark.'

The gig rattled along the well-made road at a clip. Holmes and I were furnished with travelling rugs against the evening air, and Holmes huddled in his with only the tip of his nose poking out. I wondered that he did not seek more information from Mr Week; but I did not care to tell Holmes his own business.

We turned left onto a narrower road, and continued about three more miles before turning again. 'Hold on,' called Mr Week from his platform. 'This is where it starts to get sticky.' I gripped my seat tightly, but Holmes remained as motionless as if he were carved in stone. Around us the trees formed a green tunnel, and the road seemed to blur even in the strong light of the gig-lamps. 'Misty,' shouted Mr Week. Droplets of water clung to us as the gig descended a steeper incline than any we had yet encountered, and the road began to twist and turn as it ascended. Perhaps the damp night air was getting to me, but I felt a distinct shiver pass down my spine, and drew my travel rug more closely around me.

The road curved, and the mist thickened until fat drops fell on us from the trees. 'Is it much further?' I called.

'Nearly there,' Mr Week responded. The road had narrowed to a single track, bordered by tall hedgerows; but I doubted very much that we would meet another carriage on such a night. Indeed, it felt as if we were the only people left on the face of the earth.

The road made a dog-leg, and ahead was a

sparse show of lights. 'Mickleton village,' said Mr Week, nudging the horse to go faster. I saw cottages, a church, and some long shapes which I took to be farm buildings. We left the lights behind, and the road dipped sharply. I cried out involuntarily at the drop — and then we turned a sharp left, and in front of us appeared a well-lit stable yard.

'I hope you gentlemen won't mind waiting a bit while I put up the horse and cart,' said Mr Week. 'The stable-hands are long abed.'

Holmes jumped down from the gig. I followed, more slowly. I was stiff with cold, and my old war wound ached. We stood under the eaves for a few minutes, until Mr Week had stabled the horse. 'I'll settle her properly when I've taken you two inside,' he said. 'Could you walk on the grass? The gravel is rather noisy.' I wondered at the levels of secrecy attached to the operation of bringing us to the Hall. Nevertheless, we followed Mr Week's guidance, and squelched along in the wet grass, guided by his dark-lantern.

Ahead of us a wide, low building squatted against the dark grey sky. 'This way.' Mr Week cut across the grass and led us to a small porch where a candle had been left burning. The door's paint was peeling in long strips like tree-bark. Mr Week reached into his pocket and produced a large iron key, but before he could use it the door opened inwards, silently.

'Inside, quickly!' hissed a woman's voice. 'Have they come? Are they here?'

'Of course,' whispered Mr Week, and fitted himself through the narrow gap. Holmes followed him, and I went last.

The light inside, though not strong, was bright enough after the gloom outside to make me blink. I rubbed my eyes and saw rough-plastered walls, a coat of arms over a stone fireplace, ancient oak furniture, and a rich tapestry on the wall. Yet the interior, while striking, was nothing compared to the woman standing before us, clad in a black crepe dress. She was perhaps thirty, raven-haired, and beautiful.

'Good evening, gentlemen,' she said. 'I am Mrs Holcombe. My husband awaits you in his study.'

III

Mrs Holcombe put her finger to her lips and hurried us along a corridor hung with portraits. She tapped on a panelled oak door, and stood aside.

I had last seen Bill Holcombe at school. I remembered a tall, tentative lad, his frame not filled out. The man who looked up from the fire now was a stout country squire.

'Watson!' he exclaimed. 'You've barely changed.' He levered himself from his armchair, and shook my hand. I noted his florid face, and the dark shadows beneath his eyes.

'I know,' he said ruefully. 'I have changed — but it is this business. It makes my blood run cold to think of Amelia...' He shook himself like a terrier. 'This must be Mr Holmes. I won't say I'm delighted to meet you, given the circumstances, but I sincerely hope you can help me. Please forgive my plain speech, I hardly know what I am saying.'

'It is quite all right, Mr Holcombe,' said Holmes, shaking the proffered hand.

'Nothing's all right.' Holcombe's head bowed for a second. 'But you must need refreshment after your journey. Mary!' he called.

The study door opened and Mrs Holcombe peeped in. 'Could you bring some food for the gentleman?' He turned to us. 'I am afraid it will be but a cold supper.'

Mrs Holcombe nodded, and withdrew.

'Have both you gentlemen read my letter?'

'We have,' said Holmes. 'Suppose you give us a little background, while Mrs Holcombe is engaged with supper.'

Holcombe gazed into the fire for a long moment. 'There isn't much more to tell. Amelia was the daughter of my first marriage — the first Mrs Holcombe died five years ago. She was just eleven, a bright, quick little thing, full of fun and laughter. Amelia was always delicate, and as she became a young woman it taxed her strength. You remember what a beanpole I was, Watson? Amelia was the same. She shot up, but for every inch she gained in height, she grew paler and paler. Our family physician, Dr Maloney, practically lived here, but no prescription, regimen, or tonic seemed to bring the roses back to her cheeks.' He jumped up, and jabbed at the fire with the poker. 'I apologise, gentlemen,' he said, and bit his lip. 'I am no storyteller.'

'Go on,' I said gently.

Holcombe composed himself. 'I will,' he declared. 'Amelia loved her mother dearly, and was devastated at her loss. She turned in on herself, and became wilful. I couldn't manage my headstrong girl, and she taxed her governess so much that the woman gave notice. I advertised, and was lucky to engage an exceptional candidate, with impeccable references. Amelia took to Miss Lanchester at once, and, I must admit, so did I. Our discussions of Amelia's progress grew into intimacy, and I asked Miss Lanchester to become my wife.'

'The second Mrs Holcombe?' I glanced towards the door.

'Yes. We have been married for three years now.' He sighed. 'She is so kind, so patient . . .'

'Perhaps you could continue with the narrative, before supper arrives,' Holmes prompted, gently.

'Yes. Yes.' Holcombe mopped his brow with a

handkerchief. 'Amelia seemed happier, more docile — though still not strong. I hoped she was getting over her growing sickness, although she still had a cough which concerned me, living as we do in this damp climate. I kept Dr Maloney close, and all seemed to be improving. Mary still gave Amelia her lessons, and seemed unconcerned. Then one day I came into the schoolroom. Amelia was alone, and stood to greet me. But confusion came over her face, and she sank back down. The poor child was unwell, and she had kept it from me — from all of us — because she did not want us to worry.'

'From that day I had no peace. Amelia ceased her lessons, and took to her bed. She said she had caught a chill walking on the moor — that cursed moor! We should have moved away when her mother became ill, but foolish pride stopped me. And this was the result, a poor innocent child doubled up in pain, coughing and retching and shivering. Mary stayed with her till all hours — I could not watch the poor girl suffer. But at least the end was merciful. Mary found her one morning lying in her bed, her cheek pillowed on her hand, as calm and peaceful as if she were asleep. She brought me to her, and you would not have known the child was ill. Her cheeks were rosy again, and — oh!' Holcombe choked a sob with his handkerchief. He put his head in his hands, and his shoulders shook. Holmes and I exchanged glances, and waited in silence for him to recover himself. At length he wiped his eyes, and sat back.

'I knew nothing of the — trouble — until a week after we had laid the poor dear girl to rest. I was off to the village to speak to a tenant, when Week drew me aside, and said he would go instead. I protested — I like to feel I have a personal relationship with my tenants — and asked Week his reasons. He hummed and hawed for a while, but I dragged the truth out of him, bit by bit, about what the villagers said they had seen. I could not bear to confront them myself, but I saw, when I drove abroad on business, how they shrank from the sight of my carriage, and I knew —'

'What's that?' Holmes sprang up and strode to the window.

'Did you hear something?' Holcombe seemed dazed. 'No one should be there at this hour.'

Holmes paused, his hand on the crimson velvet, then drew it aside a fraction and peered through the chink. He stood motionless for some seconds before stepping away. 'I must have been mistaken. There is nothing to see.' He smiled. 'I think the lateness of the hour is preying on our minds. I propose we retire for the night and start afresh in the morning.'

Holcombe smiled wanly. 'That seems best.' Moments later a gentle tap sounded at the door, followed by Mrs Holcombe bearing a cold collation. Holmes and I made a quick meal, while Holcombe himself took nothing, but watched us with sad, slow eyes. 'Mary will show you to your rooms,' he said. 'They are basic, but I hope adequate for your needs.' He passed a hand over his brow.

'I am sure they will be,' said Holmes. 'Mr Holcombe, do you take any form of sleeping-draught?'

'Not as a rule — Maloney has made something up for me, but I generally forget to take it.'

I stepped forward. 'As a fellow-physician, I feel you should take your doctor's advice. You don't look as if you have had a good sleep in weeks.'

'Perhaps you are right.' Holcombe stood. 'Yes, yes, I will do that.' He extinguished the lamps. 'The fire will burn itself out. Goodnight, gentlemen.'

Mrs Holcombe, candle in hand, showed us to our rooms, a pair of chambers tucked into a far corner of the house. I waited until her footsteps had died away before tapping on the connecting door.

Holmes opened it immediately, and raised his eyebrows.

'You saw her, didn't you?' Holmes's performance had been excellent, but to one who knew him as well as I did, the almost imperceptible set to Holmes's shoulders had given him away as clearly as if he had spoken aloud.

He nodded.

'What did you see?'

Holmes beckoned me in and motioned to the basket-chair, then took his seat on the bed. He spoke so low that I had to lean in to hear him. 'I heard a footstep on the gravel. I suspected a snooper, nothing more. But when I put my eye to the gap, she was standing at the edge of the lawn.' He pushed his hair back, and swallowed.

'What did you see, Holmes?' I whispered.

'A tall, slim young girl, her hair loose and flowing, dressed in a long white gown. She stood still, her arms at her sides. But her mouth and chin were smeared with blood, her dress spotted with it, and there was blood on her hands too.'

'Holmes, you don't believe —'

'She walks abroad, the letter said.' Two high spots of colour showed in Holmes's cheeks. 'The Snow-White Lady!'

I soothed Holmes, and procured a sleeping-draught from my own stock, but my mind raced as I retired to bed. Holmes was the least superstitious man I had ever met. For him to speak like this, he must have seen something uncanny. I got up to check the window catch and the door fastening several times before I drifted into an uneasy sleep.

IV

I had feared the gruesome sight Holmes had encountered the previous night would affect his health. However, he was up and about uncharacteristically early, and the faint humming from next door indicated that he was in a good mood. Presently a loud rap sounded on the connecting door, and I groaned.

'Come on, Watson!' cried a cheerful voice, followed by Holmes himself, fully-dressed. He sat on the edge of my bed and grinned at me.

I snatched off my nightcap. 'I take it my sleeping-draught worked,' I said, perhaps a little sourly.

'Like a charm, Watson.' Holmes's smile faded. 'I just hope Holcombe remembered to take his medicine, too. I suspect that if he had seen what I saw last night . . .'

'He is not strong,' I agreed.

'No. I plan to consult with the family physician today.'

'Dr Maloney?' I smiled. 'I imagine he is a good old country doctor.'

'Precisely,' said Holmes. 'It will be interesting to see you both examine the body.' I hid a shudder as he leapt up. 'I shall go and speak to Holcombe.'

He was forestalled by a tap on the door, and the soft voice of Mrs Holcombe. 'Gentlemen, when you are ready, breakfast is laid in the study.'

We sat down to bacon and eggs, and Mr Holcombe joined us. 'I have eaten already,' he said, waving away my offer of a plate. He looked tired, but less worn than he had the previous night.

'Mr Holcombe, I will get to the point.' Holmes laid down his knife and fork. 'You asked Watson here to examine your daughter, and that is the first thing we should do. I would also welcome a conversation with Dr Maloney on the subject of your daughter's health.'

'She was consumptive — she outgrew her strength —' Mr Holcombe stammered.

'I still wish to speak with Dr Maloney — in private, if I may.' Holmes's face was as impassive as a statue.

Holcombe went to the desk and scribbled a

note. 'He'll come post-haste.' He rang the bell and stepped outside with the slip of paper, closing the study door firmly behind him.

'Why is our presence such a secret?' Holmes asked point-blank when Mr Holcombe returned.

Holcombe fiddled with a waistcoat button. 'I — well — the family . . .'

'Which is more important, your family or the truth?' snapped Holmes.

'It is not as simple as that!' Holcombe cried. 'The things I have heard — I want you to set my mind at rest, but I am afraid of what you might discover!'

'What do you think we might discover?' Holmes's voice was gentler, but his eyes were fixed on Holcombe like gimlets.

Holcombe stared at Holmes, his eyes wide. '*Ruin and dishonour*,' he whispered, and staggered from the room.

***

Holmes took advantage of our time alone to make an examination of the chilly study. 'The servants need a good talking-to,' he said, running his finger along the mantelpiece and inspecting the dust. Then he seized the poker and prodded at the ashes in the grate. 'They use far too much newspaper to light the fire, when they *do* bother to light it — wait! Watson, hold this.' He passed me the poker, grasped the basket-grate, and tried to move it, but he shifted it a mere fraction of an inch. 'The tongs, Watson! No, too big.' He leaned forward until his head was almost in the chimney, and stretched a long arm to the back, scrabbling under the grate. 'Got it!' He emerged triumphant, waving a tiny scrap of newspaper in a sooty hand.

'I hope it was worth the trouble,' I grinned.

'We shall see.' Holmes peered at the fragment. 'But I can tell you that this piece of newsprint was deliberately torn this small, and it is not from any common broadsheet.'

'A local paper,' I suggested.

'Possibly, but — I have seen this type before. Oh, to be in London, within reach of my papers!' He laid the scrap in his handkerchief. 'I shall wash my hands upstairs.'

In Holmes's absence I strolled round the room. Holmes was right about the servants' carelessness, I concluded, examining the crowded flypaper. Or perhaps Holcombe was an economical man. My hand strayed to the handle of the desk drawer just as a firm knock sounded at the door.

'Dr Maloney's here as you asked, sir. Shall I —

oh!' A lad in an ill-fitting livery coat stared at me, and I daresay I returned the compliment. 'Beg pardon, sir, I didn't know Mr Holcombe had a visitor so early.' His prominent eyes ranged over me.

I assumed my best military manner. 'Show Dr Maloney in, please, then find Mr Holcombe and tell him the doctor has arrived.'

The boy raised his eyebrows at me. 'Right you are, sir.' He withdrew, and I heard an 'After *you*, sir' seconds before Holmes entered the study.

'I think our presence in the house has been noted,' I observed.

'Excellent,' said Holmes. 'I disapprove of sneaking around without good reason.'

The door opened, and Mr Holcombe entered, followed by a tall, thin, stooped man who reminded me rather of a heron. 'Dr Maloney, I presume,' said Holmes, extending a hand. 'I am Sherlock Holmes, the detective.'

Dr Maloney peered at him and nodded as he put a long white hand into Holmes's. 'Indeed, indeed. So this must be Dr Watson,' he said, turning to me and smiling even as he shook Holmes's hand. 'Always intrigued to read your cases, doctor. Although given how long the

Strand Magazine takes to reach Devonshire, I daresay I am sadly behind-hand.'

'Shall we begin, Dr Maloney,' Holmes broke in. 'I take it Mr Holcombe has explained the reason for his summons.'

'Oh yes.' Dr Maloney's expression was grave. 'A bad, bad business . . .'

'I have been invited to examine Amelia's body,' I interrupted, 'and I would welcome your professional opinion.'

Dr Maloney looked at Mr Holcombe inquiringly. Holcombe nodded, and the doctor turned back to me. 'Of course.'

Mr Holcombe walked to his desk and sat down. 'If you will excuse me, gentlemen, I have some business to attend to.' He opened the desk drawer and passed a ring with two large keys to Dr Maloney. 'I shall await your return.'

Dr Maloney led the way through the house. 'Miss Amelia is buried in the family's mausoleum,' he said, when we emerged outside. 'It is a ten-minute walk from here.'

'She died a month ago?' asked Holmes, falling into step beside the doctor.

'Yes, of consumption.' Dr Maloney was halfway down the drive when he spoke again. 'She rallied, and the family hoped for a recovery, but it was the final rally before the end. I tried to hint to Mr Holcombe, but he would have none of it. I am only relieved the shock did not kill him.' He shook his head, and strode on.

The road was as narrow and steep as I recalled from the previous night, and I do not mind admitting I was short of breath when we arrived at the brow of the hill. The church tower loomed over the village, and I steeled myself for what was to come. A few villagers raised their hats to Dr Maloney, staring frankly at Holmes and myself.

'Are you privy to the village gossip, Dr Maloney?' I asked.

Dr Maloney's face hardened. 'I do not listen to such talk, and my housekeeper knows better than to repeat such things.' He stalked into the churchyard. 'That poor girl.'

The doctor walked towards a Greek temple in miniature, set at the corner of the churchyard. Its brooding presence shaded most of that side of the churchyard. The mausoleum was guarded by tall closely-wrought iron railings, but even through those I could see crude patterns scrawled on the stone in black paint.

'Your local wise woman has been at work,'

Holmes observed. 'Those are ancient symbols, meant to keep the evil locked within,' he said to my expression of surprise. Dr Maloney unlocked the gate, tight-lipped, and we walked up the narrow path to the mausoleum. The second key slid into the lock of the iron-studded door, and turned with surprising ease.

Dr Maloney struck a match, picked up a lantern placed just inside the door, and lit the stub of candle. Then he closed the door with a clang. The lantern gave enough light to see rows of stone slabs set in the wall, carved with the names of the occupants. At the end a stone was missing, and the dark shape of a coffin stood in the niche.

Sherlock Holmes looked at Dr Maloney, who nodded.

'Why isn't she properly interred? Where is her headstone?'

Dr Maloney laughed. 'The local superstition is infecting you, Mr Holmes. The stonemason has broken his leg; I set it myself.' He led the way to the niche. 'Now, if you gentlemen will help me —' We put our shoulders to the job, and in slow increments we inched the coffin out of its niche and onto the stone floor.

Dr Maloney opened his Gladstone bag, and

extracted a small crowbar. 'Not one of my usual tools,' he remarked.

'Wait,' said Holmes. 'Doctors, what do you expect to see when the lid is lifted?'

'I expect to see a decaying body,' Dr Maloney remarked, primly. 'Dr Watson, your view?'

I cleared my throat. 'I agree with my colleague. I expect a swollen, bloated corpse. The nails and teeth should have fallen out, the hair may have followed. The skin may well have blackened.'

'Would you care to do the honours, Dr Watson?' Dr Maloney proffered the crowbar.

I stepped back. 'After you.'

Dr Maloney inserted the crowbar into the seam between the lid and the coffin. 'Draw your handkerchiefs, gentlemen, I will not answer for the smell.' The wood groaned as it lifted, and the nails bent.

'Once more,' said Dr Maloney. This time the crowbar went in at a sharper angle, and the lid rose with a crack. We all jumped back as it slid half off.

Holmes was the first to approach, and we watched his eyes widen. 'My God,' he whispered. 'Look!'

Dr Maloney and I exchanged glances and

stepped forward, prepared for we knew not what.

In the coffin lay a girl — no, a young woman. Her eyes were closed, and her cheeks flushed with a delicate pink. Her light brown hair cascaded over the shoulders of her simple white gown, and her hands were clasped in her lap.

'That is the girl I saw last night,' said Holmes. His voice had a crack in it. 'That is the Snow-White Lady.'

Dr Maloney clasped the girl's wrist for a few seconds. 'That is Amelia,' he said. 'And while she may look as if she is sleeping, she is stone dead.'

Holmes reached out and touched the girl's cheek. 'You are right. She is cold.' But as he gently put her hair aside, he moved with the caution of someone who does not want to disturb a sleeper. 'Did Amelia usually wear this locket?'

'Yes,' said Dr Maloney. 'It was her mother's, it has a lock of her hair inside.'

Holmes gazed at the locket for a moment, then lifted it from the girl's throat and peered beneath. 'Bring the lantern closer, Dr Maloney.'

The doctor obliged.

'Do you see?' Holmes pointed.

I gasped, and Dr Maloney cried out, as we saw the two little red puncture marks on the girl's white neck.

'It cannot be!' exclaimed Dr Maloney. 'There is no such thing as a vampire!'

'Normally I would be the first to agree with you, doctor,' said Holmes, and as he looked at Amelia's body his voice was as grim as I had ever heard it. 'But not today. Today I believe in vampires; and trust me, there is a vampire at work.'

V

'Holmes, what are you doing?' I half-ran by Sherlock Holmes's side in my attempt to keep up. 'What are we going to tell Holcombe?'

'Don't worry, Watson, I have a plan.' Holmes's face was set and stern as he strode down the hill.

'You're not going to tell him you think his daughter is a vampire, are you?' I panted.

Holmes stopped dead. 'Watson, do you take me for an idiot?' He glared at me for several seconds before stalking away.

'You might at least tell me your plan!' I shouted after him.

Holmes stopped again and waited for me. 'Watson, I am going to do what I should have done in the first place. I am going to run this case my way. Holcombe may be an old friend of yours, but he has been packed in cotton wool for too long.'

'Be careful, Holmes. Bill Holcombe is not a well man.'

'I am aware of that. Now, let me take the lead.'

Our footsteps crunched the gravel drive. Holmes tugged the bell-pull, and the lad in livery reappeared. 'Yes?'

'Kindly tell Mrs Holcombe that we request a few minutes' conversation,' Holmes said, in his blandest voice.

The youth nodded, and left us on the doorstep. He reappeared a minute later. 'You'd better come in.'

We were shown into a small drawing room. Mrs Holcombe was sitting on a high-backed settee. A workbox stood next to her, and a hoop with a half-finished embroidery of poppies lay on her lap. She rose at our arrival, her dark eyes wide with alarm. 'I thought you would go straight to Mr Holcombe,' she quavered. 'Is it — is it bad news?'

'Mrs Holcombe, we judged it best to speak to you first, since your husband is not strong.' Holmes's voice had softened considerably. 'May we sit down?'

'Of course.' She indicated a seat. 'I apologise, I am forgetting my manners —'

'Not at all.' Holmes sat opposite her. 'I wish to

ask you a few questions, if I may, about Amelia. I understand she was unwell for quite some time?'

'That is correct. We hoped it was just growing pains, but as you know…' Her voice faded, and she turned her head away as if in pain.

'Do you think the damp climate here had anything to do with Amelia's illness?'

A faint flush tinged Mrs Holcombe's pale cheeks. 'Yes, I do. I suggested a few times that we should move somewhere with a better climate, but my husband would not hear of leaving the Hall. He is a fresh-air, windows-open sort of man.'

'Did Amelia sleep with her window open?' Holmes was almost on the edge of his seat.

'She did — oh!' Mrs Holcombe's mouth made a little round O. 'You think something got in!'

Holmes looked at the floor and wound his watch-chain round his finger. 'I would not like to say either way,' he admitted. 'But if I could examine the room where she slept —'

Mrs Holcombe put a hand to her heart, and rose. 'Of course. Oh, my poor dear girl!'

The graceful figure of Mrs Holcombe led the way to a pretty room papered in a cheerful apple-green, though the damp had caused a few peeling corners. I took in the furnishings — the little

white bed, the dressing-table, the bookshelf —
while Holmes examined the window-catch, and
tried the window in various positions. 'How far
open was the window as a rule, Mrs Holcombe?'

'About so far.' She stepped forward and
adjusted the latch.

'I see.' Holmes regarded the gap with narrowed
eyes. 'The window faces the moors, I perceive.'

'Yes, Amelia loved the view.'

'She loved clothes, too,' I said, indicating the
framed fashion-plates on the walls.

Mrs Holcombe broke into a delighted laugh.
'She did, Dr Watson! Amelia was becoming a
young lady . . .' Her smile faded as quickly as it
had come, and she dabbed at her eyes with a
handkerchief.

'How did Amelia amuse herself, Mrs
Holcombe? You mentioned that she loved the
moors. Did she go for walks?'

'Not as much as she wanted, due to her weak
chest,' sighed Mrs Holcombe. 'She read — novels,
and poetry, and magazines — and sewed, and
played the piano. Sometimes I accompanied her to
a local dance.'

'Did she ever seem discontented?' asked
Holmes.

'No, never.' Mrs Holcombe frowned. 'Why do you ask me that, Mr Holmes?'

'I am not quite sure,' said Holmes, slowly. 'I suppose I am trying to piece together Amelia's character. Would you say she was a strong character, or a weak one, Mrs Holcombe?'

Mrs Holcombe's arched eyebrows puckered in a tiny frown. 'I would say — not weak, Mr Holmes, but easily led, as young girls so often are. But we took good care to keep bad influences at bay. We did not expose her to village gossip and nonsense —'

'I am sure you did your best,' Mr Holmes leaned forward and patted Mrs Holcombe's arm. 'It must be very difficult to take the place of a mother.' Mrs Holcombe nodded, and I looked away. I could not bear to see her cry.

'Shall I ring for your maid, Mrs Holcombe?' Holmes asked.

'P-p-please…' She buried her face in her handkerchief.

'Come, Watson.' Holmes rose. 'Mrs Holcombe, we shall return for dinner, and that is when I shall break the news to your husband. Please can you shield him until then; the truth will be hard enough when it comes.'

She nodded, and we tiptoed from the room.

'What now, Holmes?' I asked, as the front door closed behind us.

'We are going to the inn, and I am going to have a drink.' Holmes set off up the road at a stiff pace, and I trotted after him.

As we walked into the inn someone stage-whispered 'It's the detective!', followed by an immediate buzz of conversation.

'Good news travels fast, I perceive,' said Holmes, walking to the bar. 'Two pints of ale, please, landlord.'

The publican finished wiping a glass and touched his forelock. 'On the house to you, sir. How's the vampire hunt going?'

'I think we're almost there,' remarked Holmes.

'Well, the sooner she's dealt with, the better. My poor old spaniel has never been the same since she got hold of him. He shivers every time a body goes near him, so he does. A nice sharp stake through the heart, that's the thing to do, sir. An' if you don't have a stake, I'll give you the run of my woodpile with pleasure.'

'That is a very kind offer.' Holmes took a pull at his beer.

'Least I can do, sir.' The innkeeper mopped at a

puddle of liquid on the bar. 'We want people to feel they can walk home quiet-like at night, and not be huddling indoors in a quiver. And all over that flighty young piece.'

Holmes sipped at his beer again. 'Was she flighty? Her father said —'

'Her father didn't know the half of it! She'd walk down the street, nose in the air, tossing her curls at the young men, and you'd see her at the dances with her chest half-out. It's no wonder she caught a cold.'

'It was more than a cold —' I tried to interject, but the man was in full flow.

'And it ought to be too, the way she carried on! She used to be such a nice shy little thing, till the devil took her. That poor governess was no match for Miss Amelia in one of her moods.'

'Do you mean Mrs Holcombe?' asked Holmes.

'I do, begging her pardon. Now she *is* a lady.' The publican nodded with an air of finality, and wandered to the other side of the bar. 'Usual, Matt?' To my surprise I saw that he was addressing Mr Week. I raised a hand in greeting. When Week met my eye he jumped, then waved back.

'Mr Week!' called Holmes, and the land agent

walked round the bar to us. 'I did not expect to find you here.'

'Nor I you,' said Mr Week. 'I have had a long ride though, and it gives a man a thirst.' The innkeeper set a pint in front of him. 'How is the case going?'

'It is a sad business,' said Holmes, shaking his head. 'I shall have to break the news to Mr Holcombe tonight. If you could be there at dinner, he will need a friend.'

'I've worked for Mr Holcombe these last seven years, and he knows he can count on me,' said Mr Week. He cast us a look under his brows. 'It is true, then? About the . . .'

'I fear so.'

'Dear me.' Mr Week shook his head in turn, and retired to the corner.

'You are abominably slow with that pint, Watson,' said Holmes, draining his glass. 'I shall have a chat with mine host while you drink up.' He suited the action to the word, and I was treated to the sight of the publican's face frowning, then grinning, a bark of laughter, and the glint of gold as Holmes's hand moved across the bar. Holmes returned shortly afterwards. 'Are you in the mood for a stroll, Watson?'

I gaped at him, but refrained from commenting until we had left the inn and progressed some way down the road. 'What's got into you, Holmes? This morning, with all seriousness, you said you believed in vampires, and now you're cracking jokes in a public house!'

'All will be revealed, Watson.' Holmes sauntered towards the hedge and climbed over a stile. 'I have done what I can for the present; the rest will unwind later. The Holcombes dine at seven, I believe.' And with that I had to be content.

VI

We returned to Mickleton Hall at six that evening,
after a thoroughly muddy tramp through the fields.
I dreaded to think what the boots would say about
our filthy footwear, and applauded my own
foresight in bringing spare trousers.

We were approaching our rooms when Mr
Holcombe appeared at the end of the corridor.
'Gentlemen, I understand you have news for me.'

'We do,' said Holmes. 'But it is news that
cannot be delivered until dinner-time.'

'This is not a game, Mr Holmes.' Holcombe
stood firm.

'I know it, Mr Holcombe.' Holmes paused, his
hand on the doorknob. 'I have taken the liberty of
inviting Dr Maloney to dine with us tonight. I am
concerned at the effect of my verdict, and I would
be happier in my mind if your physician were
present.'

Mr Holcombe's eyes widened, but he nodded, and we gained our rooms without further interference.

Dinner was a sombre affair. All our minds were on the forthcoming revelations. Of all of us, only Mr Week made a good meal; but eventually even he pushed his knife and fork together. Sherlock Holmes waited while the plates were cleared. Then he left the room for a few moments, returned, and stood at the head of the table.

'Dr Watson and I were summoned to Mickleton Hall by an urgent letter from Mr Holcombe, asking us to investigate a case of vampirism. I am no believer in the supernatural, nor in the dark arts, but this case has changed my view.' Holmes turned towards Mr Holcombe. 'Sir, I am afraid that if you were hoping I could find an innocent explanation, you will be disappointed. I am sorry.'

Mr Holcombe bowed his head, then raised it and looked Holmes full in the face. 'I am ready,' he said, simply.

Dr Maloney half rose from his chair. 'Mr Holmes, as a scientist I do not —'

'Dr Maloney, please hear me out, and I think your scientific brain will be satisfied.' The pair locked eyes, and, muttering, the physician sat back down.

'The family presented a tale of a delicate young girl who outgrew her strength, and sadly died. The landlord of the village inn presented a tale of a flighty, vain young miss no better than she should be. Finally, we have the tale of a vampire, the Snow-White Lady, who roams at night and preys on animals — and there are witnesses who will swear to it, and produce victims. They cannot all be true — or can they?'

Holmes returned to his place, picked up his wine glass, and took a sip. 'Yesterday evening, Mr Holcombe, when I looked outside and said I saw nothing — I am afraid I lied. I saw the Snow-White Lady, standing at the edge of your lawn. A young woman all in white, her mouth and hands stained red. I will admit that the sight chilled my blood. If you had asked me at that moment, I would have said I believed in vampires. But I have an advantage over the dark side; my good, level-headed friend Dr Watson, who always sets me right. He gave me a sleeping-draught, as he recommended to you, and I woke in the morning my usual rational, sceptical self.

The next step, obviously, was to inspect your daughter's body, as you had asked Dr Watson to do. We took the precaution of inviting Dr Maloney along, and I am glad we did. Mr Holcombe, are you acquainted with vampire lore?'

Holcombe swallowed, and ran a finger under his collar. 'I am not,' he muttered. 'I do not believe in such things.'

'Let me enlighten you.' Holmes held his glass to the light, and swirled the blood-red liquid. 'Vampires are supposed to be un-dead, and if they get their fill of blood their bodies are nicely preserved. When we opened the coffin we found the body not decomposed, but as fresh as if Amelia were sleeping. And we also found two little red marks on her neck.'

Mrs Holcombe put her hands to her mouth. 'So Amelia has become a vampire!' she whispered, her eyes huge and terrified.

'No, Mrs Holcombe.' Holmes smiled. 'Again I was set right, this time by the good physician Dr Maloney. "There is no such thing as a vampire", he said. Normally I would agree, but — well, what is a vampire? A parasite which sustains itself by sucking the life-blood from another.' He put the wine glass to his lips, sipped, and set it down on the table. 'I realised that I *was* dealing with a vampire — and the vampire, Mrs Holcombe, is you.'

'Mr Holmes, explain yourself,' thundered Mr Holcombe.

Holmes pointed at Mrs Holcombe. 'Look at her, now she has been found out.'

We looked. All the sweet softness had vanished from Mrs Holcombe's countenance, and she was almost unrecognisable as the woman we had known. Her dark eyes were hard and opaque as jet, and her mouth formed a scarlet gash in her white face.

Mrs Holcombe sprang up. 'I will not stay and listen to this rubbish. How dare you accuse me!'

A smile played over Holmes's lips, but no mirth showed in it. 'Oh, you will stay, Mrs Holcombe. The servants have my express instructions to let no-one leave this room without my permission. Sit down.'

Her lip curled in a sneer. 'Let's hear it.'

'Amelia was so beautifully arranged,' mused Mr Holmes. 'Like a painting, or a stage set. And those little punctures on her neck — I suspect your sharp little embroidery scissors, Mrs Holcombe — were the final touch. But there is no such thing as a vampire. So how did Mrs Holcombe work this magic? I am afraid it is much more prosaic than a dark lord flying in the night. Amelia did not die from consumption. She was poisoned.'

'Poisoned?' cried Dr Maloney. 'But she was consumptive! I am her physician, and I know!'

'I agree, Dr Maloney. Amelia was consumptive. And when we know someone is very ill, a worsening in their health is almost expected. Now, arsenic preserves a body remarkably. I recall the case of the Styrian arsenic-eaters, whose well-preserved corpses were recognisable years after their burial. Amelia's symptoms — coughing, dizziness, flushed cheeks, cramps and retching — are entirely consistent with arsenic poisoning. First a slow, chronic dose from the beautiful bright green wallpaper — Scheele's green, indeed — riddled with damp in Amelia's room, and the bottle of skin lotion on her dressing table, of a brand containing an unhealthy dose of arsenic. Some fine ladies swear by regular small doses of the poison as a beautifier, and Amelia's pink-and-white complexion and abundant hair attest to its effect. But you were impatient, Mrs Holcombe. I saw the unchanged flypaper in the study, and I wonder if you used the rest of the packet to prepare a lethal dose. I think we will take a sample of Amelia's hair, and make sure of it.'

'How can you accuse me of such things?' wailed Mrs Holcombe, wringing her hands.

'Very easily,' said Holmes, drily. 'I read the spines of the novels on Amelia's bookshelf when I was pretending to examine the window, and found a fine lot of romantic tosh. Exactly the sort of thing to corrupt a young girl and turn her into a flirt at the least. Exactly what a conscientious governess, or a good mother, would not let her read. Add to that the fashion-plates on display, and I suspect you planned to ruin the poor girl's character in the eyes of the neighbourhood, not least in sending her to local events dressed in a way which might be acceptable in London, but seen as nigh on immoral in rural Devonshire.'

'But what of the Snow-White Lady?' Dr Maloney pressed his fingers to his temples. 'Why arrange such a ghastly spectacle?'

'I suspect Mrs Holcombe's eventual aim was to kill her husband, since I presume she is the main beneficiary of her husband's will. Amelia's death was not enough, nor the shameful village gossip about her flighty ways. Therefore Mrs Holcombe set out to produce a sight which would break her husband's heart and, in its horror, cause his death.'

Holmes whipped round. 'Ah, you are looking at the curtains, Mrs Holcombe. It is time for the show to begin.'

Holmes walked to the curtains and flung them apart, then opened the doors onto the garden. 'Remember, everyone, there is no such thing as a vampire. Ah, our heroine. I recognise her from last night.'

Before us a white figure stood in the gloom. I could just see the flowing hair and — what was she holding? 'Holmes, she has got hold of a baby!' I cried. 'Stop her!'

'Don't worry, Watson, it is in hand.' Holmes said. We watched, spellbound, as the woman bent her head over the child. When she raised it, her bloodstained lips glistened in the moonlight.

VII

The vampire was so intent on us that she did not see the dark figures creeping up till they were almost on her. We heard a scream, a whooshing sound, and then a wail as one of the men walked forward, dragging a soaked young woman holding a child's doll.

'Got her, sir,' he chuckled. 'Not much of a vampire now, is she?'

'Blast yer,' she growled. 'No job's worth this.' She threw down the doll and tried to wring out her nightgown with her free hand.

Holmes applauded. 'You were wonderful until my accomplices upstaged you, my dear. The blood is extremely convincing from a distance. May I ask — did you bite the dogs and cats, too?'

She giggled. 'Course not! I just pretended, and got a good lot of blood on their fur. Then I put 'em back where I found 'em. Funny sort of practical joke, if you ask me. And this —' She pointed to the doll lying on the grass. 'This is plain creepy.'

'Quite,' said Holmes. 'Do tell me, before you make your exit, which one of our audience hired you.'

The woman wiped her mouth on her white sleeve, leaving a dark-red smear. 'It was her.' And she pointed to the snarling, cornered Mrs Holcombe.

'Thank you,' said Holmes. 'I suggest you go and change out of your wet things, and be more careful about the work you accept in future.'

She snorted, and trudged away over the lawn. While she muttered under her breath, I caught the words 'catch my death of cold', and 'working out in the ruddy sticks' very distinctly.

'I don't understand . . .' Mr Holcombe looked pleadingly at his wife. 'Why would you do such a thing, Mary? What did we ever do to you?'

Mrs Holcombe laughed. I give her the name Mrs Holcombe, but it was as if she had thrown off a skin, and exposed her true nature. 'As the great detective says, Bill, I was impatient. God knows it's dull here, and I deserve a medal for bearing it this long. I tried to get you to move somewhere more exciting, so that I could have some sort of life — but no, the lord of the manor had to stay in his draughty old hall.' She turned to Holmes. 'But you needn't paint me as the lone villain of the piece. It wasn't just me, was it, Matthew?' Her eyes flicked in Mr Week's direction, and he held his hands up as if to ward off the devil.

'She's lying,' he stammered. 'She's trying to pull me into this to save herself. I told her about the situation, but the rest was all her idea.'

'Mr Week, it is no use trying to save your neck. You and Mrs Holcombe were partners in the exaggerated secrecy surrounding our visit. I suspected you almost from the beginning, and when I found you drinking in the public house it was clear where all those nasty rumours had originated. It isn't only Mrs Holcombe who embroiders as a hobby, is it?'

'I don't know what you mean,' muttered Mr Week, his eyes darting about for an escape route.

A chair scraped, and Dr Maloney made his way round the table to whisper in Mr Holcombe's ear. Mr Holcombe shook his head. 'I want to hear it,' he said. 'I want to hear it all.'

'You were an actress, Mrs Holcombe.' Holmes paused. 'I do not think you deserve that name.

49

What is your real name?'

'Find out yourself,' she spat.

'Oh, I shall. If I were within reach of a telegraph-office, I would already know. It was a tiny piece of newsprint which put me on your track. I knew the typeface, but I could not remember where I had seen it before. Then I met with you, and you stood, and sat, and gesticulated, and cried, just as you ought. This time, the landlord of the inn put me right. "Now she *is* a lady," he said. But you are supposed to be a governess who married well, not a fine lady — and not the heroine of a melodrama. It flashed into my head how you hit your mark every time — and I recognised the piece of newsprint as a scrap from *The Stage*. What use would anyone unconnected with the theatre have for that publication? Why would you have it now? *An advertisement*, I thought, *for an actress to play the vampire*, and the Snow-White Lady was unmasked.'

Holmes turned to Mr Week. 'I have not finished with you. I presume you knew this woman beforehand, and helped her to obtain false references when Mr Holcombe sought a governess.'

Mr Week stared straight ahead.

'It will not take me long to discover both your identities,' Holmes said. 'I promise you, you will hang.'

Mrs Holcombe stretched her hands across the table. 'Bill, if ever you loved me —'

Mr Holcombe rose abruptly. 'Do not speak to me again.' He walked over to Holmes and shook his hand. 'Mr Holmes, I am indebted to you. You have saved my life. I will leave you to do what is necessary.' Holmes accompanied him to the door, and after a hushed conversation, we heard the creak of Mr Holcombe's footsteps on the stairs.

'It grows late,' said Holmes. 'I am not sure what hours your local constabulary observe.' His mouth twisted. 'I presume no-one would care for dessert? Very well. In that case I suggest we uphold the regular custom. Gentlemen, we shall remain here while the lady adjourns.'

We gaped at Holmes, who held up a hand, and continued. 'Mrs Holcombe, there is a slight problem with your drawing room, so I have prepared an alternative. I have arranged an escort to your step-daughter's bedroom. Mr Week, as you are no gentleman, you will accompany her. We will enjoy our port and coffee, and perhaps we shall see you later.'

Mrs Holcombe got to her feet. Her eyes flashed, and her mouth was a thin straight line. 'You will burn in hell, Sherlock Holmes!'

'I doubt it,' said Holmes, mildly. 'A little too dramatic for such a small stage, my dear.' The lad in livery took her arm, and marched her to the door.

'Mr Week.' Holmes's eyes glittered. 'You will follow the lady.'

'I don't understand.' Mr Week seemed dazed. 'Why —'

'You will see. Dr Watson, would you mind showing Mr Week the way? We wouldn't want him to get lost.'

I guided the unresisting Mr Week upstairs. The servant stood by the bedroom door. 'She's in, sir. I'll stay here, just in case.'

'Thank you.' I opened the door.

The room was as I remembered it — the peeling wallpaper, the bottles on the dressing-table, the novels on the bookshelf. Yet a row of fresh new flypapers hung by the window, and a jug of water and two glasses had been placed on the dressing-table.

Mrs Holcombe was looking out of the window,

her back to us.

'The villagers are still outside,' I said.

She did not turn around. 'You haven't won,' she said through clenched teeth.

'Please,' Mr Week swallowed. 'Don't make me go in. I can't be alone with her.'

'You're a coward, Matthew,' she spat. 'I always knew it. And as usual, I shall have to do all the work.' She wheeled round, seized Mr Week's hand and pulled him into the room. 'Get out!' she screamed, and as I backed away she slammed the door in my face.

***

The decanter of port had passed round the table twice when Holmes consulted his watch. 'They have had enough time,' he said. 'I shall see if they are ready to join us. Watson, would you care to accompany me?'

'I shall come too,' said Dr Maloney.

The lad in livery was standing a few feet from the bedroom door. 'Mr Week's not well,' he said, jerking his thumb. 'He's been crying and begging to be set free, but I took no heed, just as you said.'

'Good,' said Holmes. 'And the lady?'

'Nothing. I've heard 'em moving about, and some mighty strange noises, but she hasn't said a

53

word.'

Holmes put his eye to the keyhole. 'Unlock the door, lad, and stand by the stairs.' He waited until the boy had gone before flinging the door open.

We clapped our handkerchiefs to our faces at the stench which met us, and stepped carefully over the pools of waste to the bodies beyond. Mr Week lay face-up, the handles of a pair of small scissors protruding from his neck. A pool of blood was creeping over the rug. His face was dark red and swollen, and his eyes bulged almost from their sockets. Dr Maloney went to him and gently opened his mouth with a finger.

'Asphyxiation,' he said. 'His mouth has been stuffed with flypaper.'

Mrs Holcombe had arranged herself on the bed, and an empty glass stood on the bedside table. Perhaps she had hoped to present as pretty a picture as her stepdaughter; but her face was covered in scratches, her lips drawn back in a snarl, and her hair matted with vomit.

'The Snow-White Lady is dead.' Holmes said, in a clipped, matter-of-fact voice. 'I should have known from the start.'

'What do you mean?' I asked.

'The first clue was in the letter your friend sent.

I do not know if it was Mrs Holcombe or Mr Week who named the vampire, but you will remember the tale of Snow White and her wicked stepmother.'

My eyes strayed to the damp strips of apple-green wallpaper cast onto the floor.

'Precisely,' said Holmes. 'I suggest we call the servants in to deal with this mess. Dr Maloney, will you go to Mr Holcombe and inform him that all is complete.'

'Most certainly,' said Dr Maloney. 'A clear case of death by misadventure.'

VIII

We left Mickleton Hall the next day. I was woken early by the rumble of wheels on gravel, followed by the peal of the door-bell, and peeped outside to see a plain black carriage. I kept to my room until the carriage had left.

We were summoned to a hearty meal in the breakfast room, and I was surprised to find Holcombe there before us, a cup of coffee in front of him, and an unread newspaper by his plate. We exchanged the usual morning pleasantries, and I had barely bitten into a slice of toast when the door-bell pealed again. A maid came to the door. 'Begging pardon, sir, but Mr Jeffers from the village is here, enquiring after you.'

'Tell him I'm not at — no!' Holcombe pulled the napkin from his throat and threw it on the table. 'Show him in.'

The maid bobbed, withdrew, and reappeared

shortly afterwards with the publican, holding his hat in both hands as if to protect himself.

'Our Bessie was mopping the front step when she saw the undertaker's cart go by, sir, and we were worried. My boys came back with all sorts of stories last night . . .'

'Sit down, Jeffers. Would you prefer tea, or coffee?'

The publican perched on the extreme edge of a chair, and we watched his face pale, then flush, his fist smack his palm, and his hands cover his mouth, as Mr Holcombe related the particulars of the case. 'I have told you this, Jeffers, so you can put the story straight in the village. My good name, and that of my family, has suffered long enough.'

Jeffers got to his feet, came round the table, and shook Mr Holcombe's hand. 'That I will, sir,' he said, and his voice was hoarse. 'That I will.'

'I shall rent this place, and travel,' said Holcombe, once the door had closed behind Jeffers. 'I am the last of the Holcombes, and I have been shut up here too long. If I had known more of the world —'

'Do not blame yourself,' I said. 'That infernal woman had everyone in her clutches.'

'Perhaps,' said Holcombe, 'but I should have taken better care of my daughter. She will haunt me to my death.' He stood, and shook hands with us both. 'My coachman will be ready whenever you need him. I am going for a walk on the moor.'

We were packed and ready betimes, and found the trap waiting. Our departure from the village of Mickleton was far steadier than our arrival, at the hands of Mr Week.

'Look,' said Holmes as we passed the church.

I looked where he pointed. A group of villagers, Jeffers at the head, were scrubbing the marks from the mausoleum, which was lit by the sharp rays of a fine autumn morning. 'If only all wrongs could be righted so easily,' mused Holmes, as the village vanished behind us.

***

I poked the fire while Holmes huddled in his dressing-gown. 'Your temperature is quite normal, Holmes, and I can detect no symptoms but ill-temper, which as we both know is a chronic condition of yours.'

'Be quiet, Watson, your voice hurts my head. Ring and ask Mrs Hudson for a hot toddy — quietly, mind.' He shivered. 'This is the revenge of that infernal moor. I should never have allowed you to take me on that walk.'

'Have you had your fill of adventure then, Holmes?'

'Watson, even from you that is a remark of surpassing stupidity. Pass my violin, please. I suppose you will request the *Lieder*, since you always do. Your musical diet shows an appalling lack of variety.'

The violin case lay on an occasional table, above which was a mirror, and as I went to fetch it I observed the gleam in Holmes's eyes, and the half-smile curving his lips. I made sure to keep my own expression neutral as I turned with the case in my hand, and settled on the sofa for an afternoon of music.

Sherlock Holmes and the Deathly Fog

I

The evening was impenetrable. A dense brown fog rolled over the streets of London, and its clammy fingers wormed their way into the crevices of my clothing, chilling me to the bone. If I had not known the streets of Marylebone so well, I would have had difficulty; but the cobbles fitted themselves to the soles of my boots, as if saying 'See what a match you are, sir. This is your place.'

For any other engagement I would assuredly have sent an excuse via telegram, and enjoyed a quiet evening with my wife. However, I was visiting Sherlock Holmes. It was purely a social call, to chew over old times with a light supper and a half-bottle of claret, but I would not have missed it for the world. Sherlock Holmes was not a man to be put off by fog, and therefore, neither was I.

The street lamps were faint glows amid the gloom, but I did not need them to find my way. I ascended the steps and grasped the knocker, so familiar, worn, and cool. Tonight it bore a sheen of damp. The fog had touched it, too.

But the fog had not penetrated 221B Baker Street. Mrs Hudson was as hospitable as ever, the premises as cosy and warm. Holmes himself appeared to be fighting fog with fog. He had enveloped himself in a bluish haze of tobacco, a fresh puff every so often maintaining the clouds. I knew his mood before he spoke. The slow regularity of his breathing indicated a trance-like state, and I wondered what was passing in his great brain to induce it.

'Watson,' His voice was calm, yet I started. I had not expected him to speak. 'You came.'

'Am I disturbing you?'

'Not at all.' Holmes removed the pipe from his mouth. 'It is not a three-pipe problem.' He smiled. 'Come, take a seat. I fancy Mrs Hudson will return to offer refreshment by the by.'

'I am glad you have time for me.'

The smoke had cleared enough to see the slight

twist in the smile Holmes gave me. 'Even if I were at my busiest, Watson, I would still have time for you. And I am hardly that. You would expect this vile pea-souper to bring out the villainy of the Great Wen, would you not?'

I smiled, and waited.

'You know me too well, Watson. It is the opposite. The criminal element is warming itself beside the fire, awaiting more clement weather.' Holmes's lip curled a little. He rose and poked at a log in the grate, sending up a shower of sparks.

'Or perhaps no one will venture out to report it.' I offered.

'Perhaps.' His voice was dull.

A tap at the door. 'Ah, as I predicted.'

But when Mrs Hudson entered, her usual brisk, efficient air was gone. She seemed concerned. 'Mr Holmes, someone has called to see you.'

'Really?' Holmes gazed at her with frank astonishment. 'Send them up! If they have journeyed to consult me on a night like this, I imagine it is a matter of some importance.'

Mrs Hudson fiddled with her cuff. 'I — well, yes. The thing is —'

'What is the thing?' snapped Holmes.

Mrs Hudson's eyes met his. 'This person would

never be able to pay your fees.'

Holmes waved a hand. 'That is my affair, Mrs Hudson. Please show them in. Watson and I shall make a judgement.'

II

I am not sure what I had expected, but it was not the woman sitting in the consulting-room armchair. She was perhaps fifty, stout, and florid. She reminded me of a boiled pudding still wrapped in its cloths. Her cheeks were shiny and pink, her clothes immaculate, even after passing through the conditions outside. A faint smell of soap wafted over, and with it an air of respectable, well-scrubbed wholesomeness.

Sherlock Holmes looked keenly at our visitor. 'It is a harsh night to be out, Mrs Harkness, so I presume your case is urgent. Please state your business. Beyond that you are a laundress and, from the style of your wedding ring, married quite recently, I can discover little about you.'

'I wasn't sure whether to come,' said Mrs Harkness, in a worried tone. 'Patrick — my husband — said I should leave it, and it wasn't my business. But when it's on your own doorstep, or near enough —'

'Bethnal Green?' inquired Holmes.

'Yes,' she said, with no trace of surprise. 'And with the fog an' all —' She paused, looking expectantly at Holmes.

'What does the fog have to do with it?' Holmes asked, a note of irritability creeping into his voice.

'That's when they disappear. The children.' She sighed, and her shoulders relaxed as if she had shed a huge burden.

Holmes passed a hand over his brow. 'Could you start at the beginning, Mrs Harkness?'

She nodded. 'I first noticed it at Easter, when that fog came. Thick and dark, like a sour treacle in your mouth. I shut the windows and stuffed rags in the gaps, to keep it from getting into my laundry. And it didn't,' she said, rather proudly. 'But because I was shut in for the duration, I didn't hear about young Josiah until the next day.'

'And who is Josiah?' Holmes was listening now, leaning forward in his chair, his grey eyes focused on our strange storyteller to the exclusion of all else.

'He's the boy who disappeared. The first one.

66

Eight years old. He lived in Half Nichol Street with his mum.'

'Half Nichol Street,' mused Holmes. 'Do you know it, Watson?'

I frowned. The name, while familiar, was well outside my area of medical practice. 'Isn't it part of an enormous slum?'

Holmes nodded. 'Its name is the Nichol. You live nearby, Mrs Harkness?'

She bridled a little. 'Nearby in distance, but a world away in truth. I wouldn't go into that rookery if you paid me. I only knew Josiah because he was a cheeky little scamp who'd talk to anyone. He passed my house on the way to school — when he went, that is.' She smiled fondly in recollection.

'And he disappeared?'

'His mum found his bed empty in the morning. The neighbourhood was out, shouting his name, asking everyone if they'd seen him. My Patrick said he'd probably run away, under cover of the fog, or stolen something and been took up.' She shrugged. 'But he's still missing. He would've come back, or they'd have had news.'

'Were the police called in?' I asked.

Mrs Harkness sighed. 'The Nichol isn't that

sort of place.' She looked at Holmes, doubtfully. 'I wonder if he was in the wrong place at the wrong time . . .'

'And it happened again,' prompted Holmes.

'Not till September. There were fogs, but nothing like that first one. Mists, really.' She waved a hand in dismissal of those lesser fogs. 'Then another proper beast of a fog. Liverish it was, and clinging. I kept indoors, and when I came up for air, so to speak, they were calling for Dora.'

'Another child,' said Holmes.

Mrs Harkness nodded. 'I hardly knew her, but when her brother described her — a red-haired girl in a blue pinny, with a red-haired peg doll dressed to match — I remembered. She was just six. She never came back, neither.'

She took out a dazzling lace-edged handkerchief, and dabbed her eyes. 'Even if I think I smell a fog coming on, the creeping fear takes me. It makes me glad I don't have children of my own. And now it's here again. I've been down to the Nichol and told them to keep their kids in till the fog's all gone. Some of 'em listened. Some told me to mind my own business, only ruder. So it shouldn't be on my conscience. It is, though.' She sniffed, and rocked a little. 'I nearly fell over a bunch of kiddies playing, and I told them to go home quick, but they laughed and said if the bogeyman came, they'd give him what for. I'm scared to go back, so I am.'

'Well,' said Sherlock Holmes, rising and knocking out his pipe, 'we shall accompany you. Watson, tell Mrs Hudson to expect us when she sees us.' And he took the seventeen steps downstairs at a run.

III

Sherlock Holmes fretted and muttered under his breath as the cab rolled cautiously down the main thoroughfare. 'For heaven's sake!' he cried, smacking his palm against the leather upholstery. 'Anything could be happening, and we are forced to proceed at a snail's pace!'

Mrs Harkness clasped her handkerchief to her mouth, her eyes wide.

'Try not to worry, Mrs Harkness,' I said, in my most soothing voice. 'You have done the right thing in coming to us.'

'I hope so,' she murmured, casting a sidelong glance at Holmes, who was staring moodily at the obscured street.

The cab crawled onward until it seemed as if we were doomed to journey for ever; but as we turned a sharp right, Mrs Harkness's eyes snapped open. 'Stop at Boundary Street, driver!'

'Right you are,' came the cry, followed by a hacking cough. The cab turned left, slowing to barely walking pace, before stopping outside a large building; a tavern, judging from the noise.

'You can find your way from here, Mr Holmes,' said Mrs Harkness, opening the door. 'No cab will enter the Nichol at this time, or in this weather.'

'We shall see you home, Mrs Harkness,' said Holmes, unfolding himself from the cab. 'I shall ask the cabman to wait in the pub. I doubt he will object.' He offered an arm and, after an almost imperceptible hesitation, Mrs Harkness took it.

'It is this way,' she said, pointing into the haze. Looming dark shapes were visible on either side of the road, and nothing more. I smiled as I followed them. Tall, thin Holmes and short, stout Mrs Harkness made an exceedingly odd couple.

'Oi!' A patter of footsteps followed the shout, and a small, wiry man confronted Holmes. 'What do you mean by this, sir? What are you doing?' Steam rose from him, like a horse after a gallop.

Holmes looked down his nose at the new arrival. 'Escorting this lady home. I take it you are Mr Harkness?'

The man drew himself up. 'I am indeed.' He took possession of Mrs Harkness's arm, enfolding

71

it in his somewhat shorter one, and peered at Holmes. He had to stand on tiptoe to do so. 'You're the detective, aren't you? That Holmes chap.'

'That is correct,' said Holmes.

'Well, it does you credit to come out on such a night,' Mr Harkness observed, straightening his necktie. 'I doubt you'll find anything in this fog. A fool's errand, if you ask me. Come along, Cassie.' And with a nod of dismissal, he led his wife away.

Holmes watched them vanish into the gloom. 'Hmm.'

'What is it, Holmes?' I muttered. 'Do you suspect something?'

'An interesting character,' mused Holmes. 'I wonder — but it is getting late.' He strode briskly after the Harknesses, and I had little choice but to follow. Suddenly Holmes cried out, and toppled like a fallen tree.

I hastened forward. 'Holmes, are you —?'

Two shapes were rising from the indistinct mass on the pavement. The first was unmistakably Holmes. The second was shorter, broader, and when I came closer I saw white side-whiskers. He was composing himself — settling his clothes, straightening his hat — but I had seen enough reproductions of the man to know him, though I had never encountered him in the flesh.

'Dr Parry?' I advanced, hand outstretched.

He looked up at me with bright, beady eyes, laughed, and shook my hand. 'The very same.'

Holmes, now fully upright, offered his hand in turn. 'Your zeal for health reform is famous, sir, yet on a night like this I would have thought even you would stay by your own fireside.'

Dr Parry snorted. 'This is exactly the weather when my work is most important!' He drew a test-tube from his inner pocket and brandished it. A label, writ small, had been tied round it. 'I am testing air quality,' said Dr Parry, whose small dark eyes missed nothing. 'The label denotes the postal district of London, and the street. I have collected nine samples, and was securing my tenth and last when I was rather rudely interrupted.' He cast a pained glance at Holmes.

'If you will skulk near the ground...' Holmes seemed completely unabashed.

'It's the waste of a perfectly good test tube that I most abhor,' grumbled the doctor. 'Luckily I managed to put a hand down, and saved my other samples. Now, where is my spare?' He frowned, pocketed the labelled test tube, and reached into the other side of his coat. 'Aha!' He uncorked the tube. 'Excuse me.' He executed an odd little galloping motion, scooping the test tube almost to the ground. 'There.' He corked the tube, annotated the label, and added it to his haul. 'A full set for analysis,' he said, with satisfaction. 'My work here is done.' He peered at my companion. 'And what brings the celebrated Mr Holmes to these parts?'

'Criminality,' said Holmes. 'Dr Watson and I are about to venture into the Nichol.'

'Good heavens!' said Dr Parry. 'I take it this is no run-of-the-mill matter?'

'Absolutely not,' said Holmes.

'Indeed.' The doctor buttoned his coat to the neck. 'I would invite you to supper, but as you are busy, I shall take my leave. Good night, gentlemen.' He nodded to us, and trotted away, whistling through his teeth. I eyed the swirling darkness ahead of us, and wished we were accompanying him.

'Come, Watson.' Holmes set off apace. A clock struck the half hour — I could not have said which. I sighed, and trailed in Holmes's wake.

The Nichol was no more than a hundred yards distant; but those hundred yards made a world of difference. The pavement grew irregular, as if the slabs shifted beneath our feet. The close-packed buildings sagged. Here and there one had gone, like a tooth from a rotting mouth. The air, already foul, became denser, and the fog more insistent. It whispered in my ears and insinuated its slimy touch everywhere, until I nearly choked. The street lamps ended — broken or missing, either was possible.

I could hardly see a thing. The only sounds were the whoosh of the fog moving over the earth, and our hesitant footsteps. The world had disappeared, and we were all that was left. I opened my mouth to tell Holmes that knocking on doors would be pointless, but when I breathed in the fog rushed to my brain. I doubled up in a coughing-fit. Someone shouted from above, and a dog barked.

I tried to get my breath, and the thick dark fog clogged my throat. I fell to my knees, spluttering, and then I felt Holmes's thin, strong fingers round my arm. He lifted me onto my feet, and half-carried me back the way we had come.

'Can you make it to the cab, Watson?'

'I — think so,' I replied. 'Sorry.'

We moved haltingly along Boundary Street. Every step away from the rookery made my breath a little less ragged, my footing more firm. By the time we reached the tavern I could dispense with Holmes's arm.

'Wait here,' said Holmes, putting my hand on a nearby lamp-post. 'I shall fetch the cabbie.'

The return journey to Baker Street was quicker but more erratic, which I put down to the strength of the tavern's ale. Holmes kept looking across at me, until I burst out, 'I'm not going to keel over and die, you know!'

'No…' said Holmes. 'Of course not!' he added hastily, catching sight of my expression. 'It makes one think, though.'

'It makes one think what?' I prompted, after some time had passed.

'I am not quite sure,' Holmes replied. 'But I know we have earned our supper, and I propose that you repair to your old room tonight, Watson. You should not make the journey home alone.'

As ever, Mrs Hudson provided an excellent meal, and the claret was irreproachable. Yet neither of us ate much, and the wine had to be recorked. We had both left our appetites, and much of our conversation, in that gloomy, forbidding rookery, around which the fog swirled like a disease.

IV

Sherlock Holmes crumpled the telegram in his hand and flung it at the wall. The ball of paper rebounded, skittering beneath the table.

'What is it, Holmes?' I asked, tapping the shell of my boiled egg.

'Another one,' he muttered. 'Another child gone.'

The fog had cleared overnight. When Billy came with hot water he was whistling and cheerful. 'You'd never think it had been so foul, doctor.' I blinked at the needle of light piercing the gap in the curtains.

Though the fog had departed, my cough remained. I woke thick-headed and stiff, and it took a strong cup of tea and considerable willpower to drag myself out of the warm bed. And now it appeared we were returning to last night's scene.

'Is the telegram from Mrs Harkness?'

Holmes nodded. 'She will furnish me with the details at her house. Are you fit to accompany me, Watson?'

I nodded, although I would much rather have lingered over breakfast and spent the morning in front of the fire.

'Excellent. Do buck up with that egg.'

The cab rattled along, jolting my poor head enough to make me wish the fog would return, and slow our journey. Today the streets were bright and lively; it was a different world.

'I do not see what else we could have done,' muttered Holmes.

'Don't blame yourself, Holmes,' I said. 'The Nichol was pitch black, foggy, and deserted. It might have happened before we even arrived.'

'Perhaps.' Holmes's brow remained furrowed.

Mrs Harkness lived in a terrace just off Boundary Street. I could have identified her house without the address; the knocker gleamed as if lit from within, and the windows were spotless. She opened the door to us, her eyes red-rimmed. 'I knew I should've come sooner,' she said, sniffing. 'But Patrick —'

'Never mind, Mrs Harkness,' said Holmes

soothingly. 'We are here now. Can you tell us what you know?'

'It isn't much.' She opened the door wider, and we entered a tiny hallway, then a pristine parlour. She did not speak again until we were seated on the exceedingly uncomfortable chairs.

'It's another boy,' she said. 'Harry Jones. His friends came calling for him to play, and he'd gone.'

'Where does he live?'

'Turville Street. He's about the same age as the others. Eight, maybe nine. If you listen out you'll hear 'em calling him.' Her voice cracked on the last words.

'We'll go down,' Holmes said, rising. 'Thank you for summoning me so quickly, Mrs Harkness.'

She nodded, wringing at her handkerchief, and accompanied us silently to the door.

The slum was as busy today as it had been silent yesterday, and its full horror was apparent. The houses leaned against each other like drunkards sinking to the ground. Broken windows were the rule, not the exception. Children swarmed in the courts, and played in the gutters. The smell was abominable. But in the middle of it all stood a woman dressed in black, an elaborate lace cape round her shoulders, and her face veiled. She was as still as a statue. No one touched her, no one spoke to her.

Holmes stopped a man walking past. 'Can you direct me to Turville Street?'

The man stared. 'You a copper?' His tone was not cordial.

'A detective,' said Holmes.

He jerked a thumb. 'Down there. 'Bout time they sent someone. This can't go on.' He hurried away, yelling. ''Arry? Where's 'Arry Jones?'

I looked back at the veiled figure as we walked on. She did not move. But I was sure that she had seen us, and that she had a story to tell.

'Come along, Watson,' said Holmes, striding on. 'She'll keep.'

Turville Street was as ramshackle as the rest of the rookery, and even busier with people knocking at doors and shouting Harry's name. One house, though, remained undisturbed; and it was to this house we went. An elderly woman, none too clean, opened the door, shrinking at the sight of us.

'I'm not the police,' said Holmes, putting a foot in the door before she could slam it. 'I've come to help.'

'The family's out, searching,' she snapped. 'I'm a neighbour.' She watched Holmes as if he might steal something. 'You'd best come in,' she said, at last, and opened the door an inch further. We squeezed into a narrow hall with steep stairs, lit only by a grimy window at the top. The woman nodded at the left-hand door. 'This is theirs,' she said. 'I'm over the way.'

The door was not locked. I doubt it had ever been locked; and if it had, there was little point in doing so. Hovel was too polite a term. A small square room where the floor could barely be seen; it was so crammed, with so little. A mattress lay in the corner; two more were pushed together by the broken window, and covered with ragged blankets. Two battered chairs and a table stood nearby, supporting a candle in a holder, a half-full box of wooden pegs, and a work-basket. A pile of dirty clothes climbed up the side of a small cupboard, which presumably contained everything else the family owned.

'How many children are there?' I asked the woman.

'Five,' she said. 'I hope.'

'Where does Harry sleep?'

She pointed to the mattresses by the window.

'All the children sleep there.'

A faint cry came from the doorway; a woman stood holding an infant. She was not yet middle-aged, but she appeared downtrodden, despairing, and thoroughly worn out.

'I am sorry to intrude,' said Holmes, coming forward. 'Are you Harry's mother?'

She nodded, warily.

'My name is Sherlock Holmes, and I am a detective. Mrs Harkness from Boundary Street told me about the disappearing children. When did you last see Harry?'

She swallowed, and her words came slowly. 'He was asleep with the others when I blew out the candle last night.'

'Where does he normally sleep?'

'Next the window.'

'Is the window open at night?'

'Don't need to be,' she said bitterly. 'The weather comes in as it pleases.'

Holmes went to the window and lifted the latch. It opened easily, without noise. 'Is Harry a good sleeper?'

Harry's mother shook her head. 'He's always been wakeful. I tell him to sleep or he won't get up for work. He doesn't listen. Fidget, fidget.' She sat the child on the mattress and drew a grubby sleeve across her eyes. 'Was he taken, or did he run away?'

'I don't know yet,' said Holmes. 'Do you have anything of Harry's which you could lend me? A shirt, or a sock, or a toy?'

She stared, her brows drawing together. 'Are you making game of me?'

'No, no!' cried Holmes. 'I hope to find Harry, but I require something of his to do it.'

She shrugged and went to the pile of clothes, pulling out a crumpled, grubby blue shirt. 'He was wearing this till the day before yesterday.' She gave it to Holmes. 'Please will you . . . can you bring it back, when you don't need it no more?'

'Of course I shall,' said Holmes. He inspected the shirt, and frowned. 'What does Harry work as?' The garment would have fitted the toddler playing on the mattress; not an eight-year-old boy.

'He works at Stanshall's factory, cleaning the floors and scavenging.'

'Scavenging?' Holmes frowned.

'Under the machines. Getting the dust up.' Harry's mother explained patiently. 'He's good at it 'cos he's little. He shouldn't be there, by rights, but — we need the money, and they turn a blind eye.'

'I see.' Holmes's grip on the shirt tightened. 'I shall return with any news.'

'Thank you, sir.' She nodded, and I felt her eyes on us as we picked our way out of the room and into the run-down street.

'What do you have in mind, Holmes?' I asked, eyeing the shirt.

'Exactly what I said, Watson. I am going to track Harry down, and I must engage an assistant.' He smiled at my raised eyebrow. 'Admirable as you are in many respects, Dr Watson, this assistant possesses a rare skill which you do not.'

'I have never claimed to be perfect,' I said, rather ruffled of feather. 'If I am no longer needed, I shall go home —'

'Of course you are needed!' cried Holmes, putting a hand on my arm. 'Will you stay, Watson?'

I made a show of thinking it over, more for my own self-respect than a genuine deliberation. 'If there is something useful to do, then yes.' In truth, I could not refuse Holmes, and he knew it.

'Capital,' he said. 'Talk to the mysterious woman in black. Find out who she is, why she stands there, what she makes of it all. I shall return within the hour, hopefully accompanied by my assistant.

'Anything else?' I asked, and cursed the plaintiveness which had crept into my voice.

'Talk to passers-by, if they will talk to you. Oh, and get some medicine for that cough.'

'I haven't coughed for at least ten minutes,' I protested.

'Perhaps not, but I do not like that rattle in your breathing.' Holmes smiled; his eyes did not. 'You always tell me to look after myself, and now I am doing the same for you. I would be lost without my Watson.'

I watched Holmes's tall, spare figure until he turned the corner and disappeared. This assistant could not be far away. I puzzled over his profession, since he was at Holmes's beck and call. Then again, I reflected, I was a practising doctor, and still managed to drop everything in response to a summons from Holmes. I allowed myself a rueful smile that I was not the only one. Yet why had I never encountered this skilled individual before?

A rush of noisome wind recalled me to my duty, and I shook myself impatiently. Holmes could associate with whomever he liked; I had work to do.

I strode purposefully back to the court we had first halted in. She was still there, veiled and motionless. I blew my nose, settled the points of my waistcoat, and straightened my tie. I felt unaccountably nervous. But approach that black figure I must, and approach her I would. I cleared my throat one last time, and walked towards her.

V

'Let them go.' The woman's voice rang out, and again I wondered how she had come to such a place.

'What do you mean, madam?'

'Let the children go. The fog has taken them. They have not been found, therefore it is God's will. It must be.'

'Do you really believe that it is the fog?'

Her eyes burned through her veil. 'Look around you, sir. All are searching, but will they find the latest child to disappear? No. Their shoulders are bowed already. They are defeated. How can they fight a deathly fog?'

I shivered as I remembered the way the fog had clung about me. My throat tightened, and I began to cough.

'Even the memory of it affects you. It takes whom it wants. The night after the fog took Josiah

87

I stood outside until dawn. I hoped it would take me, too. The fog wants to take you. I feel it.' She flung up her veil and leaned forward, as if to see me better. Her dark eyes were hot coals in her white face. She was under thirty, and might have been pretty if she were not so pale. 'You and your friend should go away. This is not your sort of place. Policemen and officials do not belong here.'

'Perhaps we ought to,' I said. I wished Holmes had not left me. 'Are you Josiah's mother?'

'I was.' She spoke without emotion. 'I am nobody's mother now.'

'You believe he is dead?'

'Yes, and there is nothing I can do about it.' Her words were hard as flint.

'Well, Holmes and I are going to try.'

'Sherlock Holmes?' Her eyes widened.

'You have heard of him, madam?'

'Then you must be Dr Watson.' She considered me. 'I read your adventures in the *Strand*. At the public library,' she added. 'If I could afford to buy the *Strand Magazine* I would not be living in the Nichol.' She gazed past me, her lip curling.

'You do not belong here, either.' An impulse came over me to take her hand and lead her out of this run-down maze; to take her for walks, to dinner, to the theatre. To amuse her, to divert her, to make her better though she was not ill —

'I do now.' And that was the end of it.

'Excuse me for asking, madam, but have you seen anything — unusual?'

'When the fog comes?' Her mouth twisted into something like a smile. 'I stay out as long as I can bear. I hear the swirl of the fog, occasional footsteps, the grind of cab wheels and the clop of horses. But I see nothing. I am no use to you or your companion, Dr Watson. I am sorry.'

I extended a hand. 'It may prove useful, madam. Thank you.' Her grasp was firm within her slippery, cool black glove. I turned once, at the boundary of the slum; she still watched me.

It was a relief to leave the rookery, and her. I felt as if I had been scrutinised under a microscope. I wondered where she came from, and how she had ended up living there. Some wastrel husband, no doubt, or worse. I smacked my fist into my palm, which earned me a frown from a matronly woman carrying a wicker basket. I crossed the road to avoid further censure, and saw the familiar druggist's bottles ahead of me. A refuge.

The bell jangled, and a dapper little man with a

waxed moustache advanced. 'Good morning, sir. How may I help you?'

'I have a chesty cough; I suspect the recent fog has caused it. A bottle of Owbridge's lung tonic should see it off.'

'A foggy cough, eh? Try this.' The druggist turned to the shelf behind him and took down a small squat bottle, its label thickly printed. 'It's very popular.' He passed me the bottle.

'Professor Wellman's Cough Soother,' I read. 'What's in it?'

'Oh, the usual. Alcohol, a spot of laudanum, a smidgen of cannabis, plenty of sugar, aniseed oil for flavour, and a few herbs, well-drowned in water.'

'It sounds all right, but does it work?'

'Most of my regulars swear by it.' The druggist waved his hand at the row of bottles.

'I'll try a bottle. How much?'

'A shilling, which is good value. If I mixed the medicine myself I'd have to charge more.'

I slid a shilling across the counter, then peered at the bottle. 'A small spoonful twice a day till the cough is gone,' I read.

'That's it. Make sure you shake the bottle, though. Otherwise the good stuff sinks to the bottom. Good day to you, sir.'

I paused on the step of the druggist's and shook the bottle thoroughly before uncorking it and taking a small dose. The aniseed flavour, while strong, was not unpleasant, and the liquid wrapped my throat in warmth. My breathing seemed easier, too. I pushed the cork home —

'Drinking in the street, Watson?'

I nearly dropped the bottle. 'Holmes, I am merely following your advice —'

My jaw sagged.

Holmes was not alone. A gigantic hound stood next to him, its great sad eyes fixed on me. It was the biggest bloodhound I had ever seen.

'So this is your assistant,' I said, weakly.

Holmes smiled. 'Chudleigh, shake hands.'

The hound offered a huge chestnut paw, and I shook it gingerly. It was very different from the previous silken handshake.

'Now you two have met, we can get down to business.' Holmes strode towards the Nichol, and Chudleigh loped beside him, his lead slack. 'Come on, Watson.' I hastened to catch them, feeling something between relieved and relegated.

A few minutes later we were outside the house in Turville Street. Holmes pulled Harry's little shirt from his pocket and held it to the dog's nose. 'Seek, Chudleigh! Find him!'

Within seconds the bloodhound put his nose to the ground beneath the broken window. Holmes glanced at me, triumph in his eyes. 'At last we are getting somewhere.' Chudleigh turned, almost knocking Holmes down. He barked once, and crossed the road, towing Holmes behind him.

We followed the hound straight as an arrow along streets and alleys, barging pedestrians, calling apologies in our wake. Finally we emerged at Brick Lane. Chudleigh turned right, and led us perhaps another couple of hundred yards before stopping so suddenly that I nearly fell over him. He sniffed the ground and started down an alley, then backed out and sat, gazing at Holmes.

'Good dog, Chudleigh,' said Holmes, patting him on the head.

I surveyed the scene. It was a busy place. Shoppers with baskets hurried past knots of children playing in doorways. Men dressed for business strutted by, knocking at doors. Above our heads rose the clank of looms, and an occasional shout which sounded like an order. I strolled down the alley Chudleigh had explored. It led to a large building, its windows too grimy to see inside. A brass plaque stated *Jenner and Sons, Manufacturers. Visitors by appointment only.* An odd, sweetish smell hung about the place, and smoke issued from the tall chimneys.

Holmes sniffed the air. 'Hmm. Raspberryish. A hint of liquorice, too.' He scanned the brass plate, and snorted. 'The trail has gone cold. I suspect whoever took Harry had a carriage waiting here.' He gave Chudleigh another sniff of Harry's shirt, but the hound did not resume the chase. 'My assistant has done his best, and I shall take him home. He has a show tomorrow, and it was all I could do to secure him.' He turned down a side road.

'Is that it?' I asked.

'What else would you have me do, Watson?' His voice was not raised, yet it cut like a knife. 'These are preliminary skirmishes. I do not intend to give up.'

'Oh,' I said. 'I thought —'

'I will not be beaten by a fog,' Holmes said, through gritted teeth. We turned onto Commercial Street and Holmes hailed a cab. 'Go home, Watson.'

'Don't you want me to return to the Nichol?' I said. The words came out sounding rather more injured than I had meant them to.

Holmes opened the door of the cab and Chudleigh ascended the steps. 'We have been seen enough there today. I shall think things over. If I need you, I shall wire.' He followed Chudleigh into the cab and closed the door. 'Finsbury, please.' Chudleigh barked once as the cab moved off, and within seconds they were lost amid the other traffic of Commercial Road.

I sighed, and — how wonderful — I did not cough. The patent medicine was surprisingly effective. Still, perhaps Holmes had a point. Now that I was unshackled from the fog, I had patients to attend to. I signalled the next cab, and gave my orders for Paddington.

I marvelled at how well I felt — the lassitude, cough and thick-headedness were gone. I would never be as sharp as Holmes, of course; but I was back to my old self. Indeed, a few of my patients were suffering with a cough, and I recommended Professor Wellman's mixture to them, citing my own rapid improvement. *What a happy accident*, I thought, in a rare moment of quiet between patients.

I was kept busy until five o'clock, and on reaching home my wife and I had so much to talk about that I almost forgot my second dose of the Cough Soother. I was climbing into bed when I remembered the squat dark bottle in my coat pocket. Should I bother? After all, the cough had not returned. The doctor in me, though, argued that a second dose might vanquish the irksome cough completely.

'What is it, John?' called my wife.

'Just a moment, Mary.' I padded off, retrieved the bottle, and went to the kitchen for a spoon. I smiled to myself at how I must have looked, swigging the mixture on the druggist's step. I shook the bottle, poured a scant spoonful — no point wasting the stuff — and drank it.

The effect was less pronounced than before, but I felt better. There. I corked the bottle and smiled at it, turning it to read the ingredient list. Just as the pharmacist had said; good, honest, tried-and-tested . . . My eyes scanned down the label to the bottom. A slogan in bold capitals, SOOTHES LIKE NO OTHER, and underneath, the manufacturers.

Jenner and Sons, Brick Lane, London.

VI

My wife sat bolt upright in bed at the sight of me. 'John, whatever is the —'

'I'll explain later.' I flung on a shirt and trousers, thrust my bare feet into shoes, and ran downstairs.

The telegraph office at Paddington Station would be open, and it was a short cab ride away. I composed a quick wire to Holmes: *Cough mixture mfrs JENNER Brick Lane surely no coincidence Watson,* and handed it in at the desk.

The clerk ran a slow pencil under my words, mouthing them to himself. 'You haven't used all your words, sir.' He looked up. 'You could add another ten, you know. It doesn't cost any more.'

'It's fine as it is,' I said. 'Just send it, please.'

He raised his eyebrows. 'Any reply?'

'I'll wait.'

He indicated a bentwood chair in the corner

and sauntered into the back office, slip in hand. Two minutes later he resumed his seat, staring at the lamp.

I examined my fingernails and wiggled my toes in my shoes. Surely Holmes was not asleep. Billy would wake him. He would read the telegram, and jump to the same conclusions as I had. I watched the minute hand of the clock tick round several times before I accepted that there was no reply. Holmes must be out. I rose, said goodnight to the clerk, and caught a cab home. I had done my best to reach Holmes, and I could do no more until morning. Yet I went upstairs with a heavy heart, and gave the briefest of explanations to my wife before settling to a fitful sleep.

I awoke sticky-eyed and fatigued. It was still dark.

The bell rang again.

'I'll go,' I said, to no-one in particular, and threw off my sweaty covers. I tied the knot of my dressing-gown firmly and padded to the front door.

A blue-overalled, unshaven man stumbled in, his big boots scuffing the tiles. He stank of beer, and had clearly spilled a quantity over himself. His hair stood on end, and dirt streaked his face. I closed the door, and by the time I turned back to the man he had resolved himself into my old friend.

'What have you been up to this time, Holmes?'

'Making the acquaintance of some inhabitants of the Nichol, by way of the tavern.' Holmes rubbed his cheeks, leaving them dirtier than before. 'It was an enjoyable, yet unprofitable evening, since most of them were too drunk to talk sense. Our friend Patrick Harkness arrived early; I took particular care to listen to him. Unfortunately his conversation concerned a hot tip for the two-thirty at Newmarket, and how to get the money from his wife.' Holmes's mouth twisted. 'I stuck it out, in the hope of eventual *in vino veritas*, and wended my way home in the small hours. There I read your telegram, and here I am.'

I examined Holmes more closely. His eyes were red-rimmed, and beneath the dirt his face was pale. 'You haven't slept, have you? What time is it?'

'No, and close on five o'clock. These drinking men keep long hours, whatever the licensing laws may say.'

I rubbed my eyes. 'What is the plan, Holmes?'

'Honestly?' He smiled. 'My first thought was reassure you that I had read your message. My next thought was strong coffee and exceedingly hot water; I feel filthy inside and out. And my third thought was to break into Jenner's factory. I do not understand the connection, but as you so rightly deduced, Watson, it is surely no coincidence.'

'What are you two whispering about?' My wife stood on the landing, her dressing-gown wrapped round her. 'Mr Holmes, it is a little early for a social call.'

Holmes bowed; a comical sight, given his appearance. 'I do apologise, Mrs Watson —'

'I know,' she said, in a resigned tone. 'You're on a case.' She sighed. 'I suppose you want coffee.'

'Actually,' said Holmes, 'I am not sure that I do.' He opened the front door. 'Look!'

I peered out. It was still dark, as I expected — in late October, the sun did not rise until past seven. But it was a thick, glutinous darkness, and the street-lamp showed a faint, obscured glow.

'The fog!' I whispered. 'It is coming down again.'

'I felt it as I climbed your steps — I did not expect it to settle so quickly. There is no time to lose, Watson!'

I sprinted upstairs, threw on my clothes, and fetched my army revolver, loading it with quick, shaking hands. 'One moment,' I panted. I ran to the kitchen, grabbed the bottle of Cough Soother, and stuffed it into my overcoat pocket.

'Ready?' asked Holmes, eyebrows raised.

'Ready.'

'Then let us go.'

Holmes hailed a cab. 'Old Nichol Street, please.'

'Not at this time of night,' the cabman retorted.

'I'll make it worth your while.' Holmes held up a sovereign. 'If you're quick.'

The cabbie clicked his teeth, and jerked his head towards the cab. 'Garn. You'll be me last fare, I reckon. Might as well have something to show for the night.'

'I don't understand,' I said, as the cab growled over the cobbles. 'Aren't we going to Brick Lane?'

'We are,' said Holmes. 'But I must engage an assistant first.'

'Not another dog,' I muttered.

'I just hope we are not too late.' Holmes fidgeted and peered at the descending fog.

The cab lurched and galloped as I told Holmes of my encounter with the veiled stranger. The cabman, having agreed to risk his life by entering the Nichol after dark, seemed to have thrown caution to the winds. We arrived within twenty minutes. Holmes jumped down and handed the cabman a sovereign. 'Wait a few minutes, and there'll be another.'

'Aye, sir,' said the cabman, far more cheerfully.

We ran into the heart of the rookery. 'Who are we looking for?' I asked.

'The woman in black,' replied Holmes. 'Quietly, now.'

We crept along, handkerchiefs to mouths to keep the worst of the fog out. The slum was quiet, and the fog not yet at full strength. I peered into the court where she had stood, and — yes! I pointed to a slim, dark shape.

'Well spotted, Watson. I shall go and talk to her.'

'Dressed like that, Holmes?'

'Good point. She knows you. Here's what I want her to do.' Holmes delivered the message under his breath. 'I'll wait.'

I raised a hand in greeting. I knew from the slight motion of her shoulders that she had seen me, but she made no further sign until I stood before her.

'You have returned with the fog, Dr Watson.'

'I have,' I said. 'And you can help us.' I leaned down and whispered in her ear.

She frowned at me. 'Is this some sort of joke?'

'I was never more serious in my life,' I said. 'I must go. If we are right, I hope to meet you again soon.' I pressed her hand, and hurried back to Holmes.

'Do you think it will work?' I asked, as the cab pulled away.

'There's only one way to find out,' said Holmes. 'And now for a spot of burglary.'

VII

'You're sure no-one's here?' I asked, glancing along the alley.

'On the contrary,' said Holmes, setting his jaw as he worked on the lock. 'I hope to find three people. At the very least.' He selected another pick. 'Aha!' he muttered at the click. He applied light pressure to the door, and it opened inward. 'Now we shall see.' He closed the door behind us, and presently I heard the *rrrrrrip* of a match striking. Holmes shielded the flame, and we inspected our surroundings.

We were in a hall with several glass-panelled doors leading off. The first office was the clerk's, and there we found a candle, just as Holmes's match began to fade. 'The fates favour us, Watson,' he smiled.

We passed from room to room; a larger, more elaborate office labelled *Director,* with sample medicine bottles in a cabinet; a cloakroom; a kitchenette. 'What are you looking for, Holmes?'

'A locked door,' he whispered. He tried the door marked *Works*. 'We are getting somewhere.' The lock-picks came into play again, and we entered a huge room crammed with equipment. Holmes walked quickly past the long tables, the huge vats, the cupboards full of bottles. 'This is not it.' I followed him to the door at the end, trying not to wince at the noise of our footsteps. I was sure my heart could be heard in the street.

Holmes turned to me. 'Before I go on, Watson, you must return to the hall. Detain whoever enters; shoot them if you must. I shall accompany you.'

I nodded, and swallowed. Holmes walked back with me and relocked the front door. 'That should give you fair warning,' he said. 'I shall continue my quest. When you have them, shout.'

'I will,' I said, hoping I was as brave as I sounded.

'I know you will.'

Holmes retreated, the light travelling with him. He closed the factory door, and I was plunged into a darkness which became thicker every second.

I took out my revolver and checked each

cartridge. I stood ready, and counted a minute in my head.

Nothing happened.

I counted another minute, and another. I considered sitting down. It would be hard, cold, not much better than standing. Perhaps if I leaned on the door . . . I let my head rest on the wood.

The door rattled, and my heart caught in my throat. I stepped away, raised my gun, and waited.

Scuffling outside, and muttering.

Please don't let there be two of them. Or more. I longed to summon Holmes, but it was against my orders.

A key in the lock.

Click.

The door opened. I could just see the shape of a top hat. The figure stooped. A small *ugh* of breath, and it straightened. He was carrying something. Something quite large.

I moved further back, hardly daring to breathe, as the man stepped over the threshold. He stooped again to release his burden, then turned the key in the lock.

I aimed for the wrist, and cracked the gun down with all my force.

'Aaagh!'

'Holmes! Holmes!' I cried. I reached out, catching a lapel. 'Don't struggle, or I'll shoot you.'

A kick on my ankle bloomed sharp pain. 'Holmes!' I shouted, and grabbed the darkness, securing an arm this time.

Hammering at the door. 'Let me in!' A woman's voice. Her voice.

A dim light, growing stronger. Holmes flung open the door, and his face changed before my eyes. It had been full of righteous fury, but now the predominant emotion was astonishment. 'You!'

I pulled the man round to face me.

My eyes met Dr Parry's. And lying at his feet was an unconscious, ragged little girl.

VIII

'I am surprised to see you, Dr Parry,' said Holmes.

'And I you, Mr Holmes. Especially in such a state of disarray.' Dr Parry had already recovered his composure, and twinkled at Holmes in the manner of a jolly old uncle. 'You have found my workshop, I perceive.'

'Yes, and I have also found your experiments.' Holmes pulled a small pistol from the inside of his overall. 'Now Watson and I are both covering you, so I trust you will behave yourself.'

'Do I have a choice?'

Holmes motioned Dr Parry aside and unlocked the door. The hammering ceased, and the woman in black stepped in. Her eyes roved between the three of us. 'You were right.' Her voice was quiet. 'A delicious smell, like the best sweet shop there ever was. Fruit, sugar, and toffee, all mixed together. I followed it, keeping in the darkest places. I heard a scrape, then a creak, then light feet following where the smell led. It led us here.' She looked down at the child sprawled on the floor. 'What have you done to her?'

'She is perfectly well,' snapped Dr Parry. 'Merely sedated.'

I knelt and sniffed, keeping my gun trained on Parry. 'Laudanum, I assume.' I got up and produced the bottle of Professor Wellman's Cough Soother from my pocket. 'You have experience with it.'

'Indeed I do,' said the doctor, completely unabashed. 'She will wake in a clean bed, wearing new clothes, probably for the first time in her miserable little life. She will enjoy a good breakfast, toys, and the company of other children. All I ask in return is a little assistance.'

'Where are they?' Josiah's mother caught his arm. 'Where are the children?'

Dr Parry eyed her hand on his sleeve. 'And what business is it of yours . . . madam?' He coughed the word up like a fishbone.

'Children are missing,' she growled. 'My son is missing, and it is your doing!'

Dr Parry shrugged. 'They are happy. If you

asked them, they would not want to go home.' His lip curled. 'Come and see them, then tell me I am doing wrong.' He advanced to the door marked *Works*, and beckoned us on. 'Leave that one sleeping. I shall come back for her, once you are quite satisfied.'

'This might be a trap, Holmes,' I muttered.

'I have already seen them,' said Holmes. 'Through the keyhole.'

Dr Parry led the way across the workroom and opened the far door. 'You have preceded me, Holmes.' His tone was one of amiable surprise.

The door led to another hall, and a staircase. Dr Parry pointed downwards. 'Into the bowels of the earth,' he grinned. We descended two short flights and he opened a plain wooden door to reveal yet another hallway. The layout mirrored the floor above; but the door corresponding to the *Works* door had no glass panel. The doctor smiled, shaking a ring of keys. 'Here we are!' He unlocked the door, and flung it open to reveal one of the strangest sights of my life.

Within the room was another room made entirely of glass, the gas-lamps turned low. It was fitted with child-sized furniture; a table and chairs, a blackboard and chalk, a miniature chest of drawers, and three little white beds. It was a doll's house with living occupants, though at this moment they were either asleep or unconscious. And also asleep, on a chair outside the well-sealed door of the glass room, was Patrick Harkness.

Two of the beds showed the humped covers of a sleeper. The last bed was empty.

The woman in black pushed forward and put her hands to the glass. 'Three are missing. Where is the other?'

'Please do not wake the children,' said Dr Parry, smoothly. 'They will be tired if they are not rested.'

She beat the glass with her fists. 'Wake up! Wake up!'

'Kidnapping is a crime, Dr Parry,' said Holmes.

Mr Harkness mumbled in his sleep. I leaned in to catch his words. 'Noisy children. Make 'em sleep. Good an' proper.' He snorted, his head rolled round, and he settled again.

'Not the best watch-dog,' commented Holmes. He turned to Dr Parry. 'So these children are your guinea-pigs, lured into your glass prison by the promise of a treat.'

'That's it.' Dr Parry took a large bottle from his pocket — it resembled an oversized perfume bottle — and squeezed the rubber ball attached to it. At once the air filled with a wonderful smell of strawberries and caramel. Saliva sprang to my tongue. 'Once this gets in at a child's window, they'll follow it anywhere. That's the beauty of getting my children from a rookery. The children are starving, the windows are broken, and no one will dare to summon the police.'

Josiah's mother paused in her banging. 'Why won't they wake up?'

'A mild sedative is piped into the room,' said Dr Parry. 'Also, the glass is tempered. You'll have to work much harder than that to rouse them.'

'I understand now,' I said. 'You pipe in the fog to make them ill, then refine your medicine to cure them.'

'Exactly, doctor,' smiled Parry. 'Not just one fog, either. I collect air samples from various districts, reproduce them in my laboratory, and adjust the mixture to the optimum levels for each area. Localised cures!'

'How many children have you stolen?' Holmes asked, bluntly.

'Not *stolen*.' The doctor shook his head in pity at our lack of comprehension. '*Borrowed*. Four, counting tonight's. The idea came to me recently,

111

you see, and there is only room for three. Though if the medicine continues to fly off the shelves, I could move to larger premises —'

'Where is the other child?' Josiah's mother rounded on him. 'Which one is not here?'

'There was a slight mishap.' Dr Parry waved a hand. 'It does not do to dwell on minutiae. Are you acquainted with the work of Jeremy Bentham, Mr Holmes?'

'Of course.' Holmes frowned.

'Then you will appreciate my argument,' beamed Dr Parry. 'The greatest happiness of the greatest number — that is the thing. The children are happy, as their living standards are vastly improved. The public is happy, since it can be cured of all manner of respiratory illness at a very reasonable price. I am happy, for at last I have money to pursue my research, without constantly having to beg to the great and the good.' He spread his hands. 'Who could ask for more?'

The woman in black moved to my side. 'Make him answer,' she pleaded, her dark eyes shining with unshed tears.

'Dr Parry.' I motioned with my gun. 'Please answer the lady. Where is the other child?'

Dr Parry sighed. 'One child. One wretched

guttersnipe. Is that what all this is —'

She wrenched the gun from me and fired it at the bottom of the glass door. Her boots crunched on the shattered fragments. She pulled down the first blanket, uncovering a red-haired girl. In the second bed, a blond boy. She stared at the third, empty bed. 'Where is he?' she cried. 'Where is Josiah?'

'In a better place,' said Dr Parry. 'As he has been ever since I borrowed him.'

'He's dead, isn't he?' She raised the gun, and aimed it at Parry. 'He's dead.'

Dr Parry began to lift his hands, and, with a faintly apologetic look, opened his mouth to speak. But she did not wait to hear him.

Parry staggered backwards, and the sound of the gunshot reverberated into silence. His expression did not change at the sight of the blood soaking his shirt-front, and he made no attempt to staunch the flow. 'No medicine . . . will cure me now,' he said conversationally. His legs gave way under him, and he crumpled to the floor. 'See what you did.' He coughed once, a strangely dry, precise little cough, and that was the last we heard from Dr Parry.

'Bloody hell.' Patrick Harkness croaked,

putting a hand to his head.

I stepped through the shards of glass to the children, who were turning this way and that, as if waking from a long sleep. Their foreheads were warm, but not unduly so, and their pulses, while slow, were within normal range. 'They need a thorough examination. For now, though, getting them home is more important.'

'The missus is going to kill me,' whimpered Harkness.

'You should have thought of that sooner,' said Holmes. 'Before you got involved with this racket. Before you married her, even.' He turned to the woman in black. 'Madam, give me the gun.'

She stared at him, my revolver dangling from her fingers. 'What will you do? Arrest me?' Her cheeks were flushed, her eyes bright. 'Follow your heart; that's what the stories say. I followed my heart when I took up with Josiah's father, and my family disowned me. He left, and Josiah was all I had. Everything I endured — every humiliation, every hardship — I bore for my son's sake. And he was taken, too. I have been punished enough, and I will not stay for more.' She raised the gun and put it to her breast, and her eyes blazed a warning. I wanted to turn away, to not see it, but I could not break her gaze. I could not leave her in that final moment. The gun spoke again; and it proclaimed the end.

IX

It was a long, long morning. Holmes went to fetch a policeman, leaving me to guard Harkness. It was an easy task; all the bumptiousness had leaked out of him, and he slumped on his chair like a broken puppet. Holmes returned a few minutes later, followed by a policeman who reeked of brandy. 'It's only to keep the fog out,' he protested.

'Make yourself useful and watch this little lot,' said Holmes. 'I'm wiring Scotland Yard.'

Inspector Gregson arrived with reinforcements, and whistled as Holmes delivered an edited version of the night's events. 'This will put the cat among the pigeons,' he said. 'Dr Parry was a notable fellow. What about these kids?' He glanced at the makeshift tent of sheets and blankets which, to his credit, Harkness had rigged in a corner of the glass box. From inside came snatches of a hymn, sung by one deep voice and two little piping ones.

'We'll take them home,' said Holmes.

And so Holmes and I escorted the children, clumsily dressed by Harkness, back to their families. The fog was lifting already, and the sky brightening. Holmes held the hands of Harry and Dora and I carried the last little girl, who gazed around her with enormous brown eyes and giggled at being so far from home. We knocked at Harry's door, and his mother nearly dropped the toddler in her astonishment. She put it down and clasped Harry to her. He twisted round and stared at us, his face confused. 'No sweets no more?' he said. 'No toys?' And he began to sniffle.

'It's a long story,' said Holmes to Harry's mother, who now looked as confused as her son. 'We will return, and try to explain.'

Dora bawled when we handed her over, scrubbing her fists into her eyes. We shook our heads as we walked out of the Nichol, and onto Boundary Street.

Mrs Harkness received our news without tears. 'I'm glad you found them, and I'm so sorry for little Josiah,' she said. 'I wish…' Her hands twisted at the bright white handkerchief in her lap.

'Do you think she knew?' I asked, as we

walked along the street.

Holmes considered, hands in pockets. 'She would have gone straight to the police if she had known. I suspect Harkness talked in his sleep, or in his cups. Perhaps she was asleep too. But she sensed something wasn't right, and she came to us. I just wish —' He broke off too, and looked at the pavement.

We were quiet on the journey back to Baker Street. 'Will you come to breakfast, Watson?' asked Holmes, as the cab slowed.

'Thank you, Holmes, but no. I shall go home and sleep.'

Holmes nodded. 'A wise decision. Once I am cleaned up, I shall sleep too.' He shook my hand before jumping down. 'Watson —' He leaned on the window-sill.

'Yes, Holmes?'

He opened his mouth to speak, and a shadow crossed his face. 'Don't be a stranger too long.' He turned, and ran up the steps to 221B Baker Street.

'Paddington Station,' I said to the driver. I could walk from there, and perhaps the fresh air would do me good.

'John! Where have you been?' My wife ran into the hall. 'You look exhausted.' She helped me off with my coat. 'This is very light . . . where is your revolver?'

'At the scene of the crime,' I said, wearily. 'I don't want to talk about it, Mary. All I want to do is sleep.'

Mary put her arms round me and held me close. She smelt of fresh linen, lavender-water, and normality. 'Then go and sleep.' She led me upstairs, found a fresh pair of pyjamas, and turned down the bed.

I shuddered. It was too like the neat, clean children shut in their glass-house. I opened the curtains, and raised the window-sash to let in fresh air and noise. Mary raised her eyebrows as I climbed into bed, but said nothing, leaning over to kiss me goodnight.

'Mary . . . do I ever talk in my sleep?'

A little frown. 'No, John, never. Why do you ask?'

I closed my eyes and saw her flushed face, her bright eyes, her silk-gloved hand, the way she had flung up her veil to look at me.

'No reason, dear. Just a thought.'

The Case of the Curious Cabinet

I

It felt as if the Indian summer would never break. London baked in the heat. The close-packed buildings offered no shade or respite, reflecting the sun back onto the journeyman pedlar and the City gentleman alike. We were all ants trapped under a common magnifying glass.

The black front door of 221B Baker Street seemed to glow, and the brass knocker was almost too hot to handle. Yet handle it I must; for Sherlock Holmes had summoned me. His wire had arrived via a perspiring telegraph-boy. *An adventure beckons stop 221B post-haste SH.*

Even the usually unflappable Mrs Hudson appeared hot and bothered, though pleased to see me. 'It's this heat,' she said. 'It gets to me, Dr

Watson. And to Mr Holmes, too.'

'I didn't think Holmes was affected by any external circumstance whatsoever,' I joked.

'It's not the physical effect,' she said, darkly. 'The weather hasn't broken all summer, and it's as if...' She led the way upstairs. 'You know his experiments?'

'Oh yes.'

'Sometimes I've come in when he's been heating a flask of liquid. First it bubbles a little, then harder, until the bubbles are at the top of the flask, and you can't tell whether it's going to spill over or boil dry.'

'Mm.' We reached the landing. 'Very interesting, Mrs Hudson,' I commented, striving to be polite to my former landlady.

'I just can't tell which way he'll go,' she muttered. 'He needs a break in the weather, and so do we all.' She knocked at the consulting-room door, announced me, and left without another word.

'Mrs Hudson is concerned, I perceive.' Holmes was standing at the window, a letter in his hand. 'It is no great deduction, Watson. She looks at me as if I were a volcano that might erupt at any instant.'

'She worries about you, Holmes.'

'I know. But there is no need. Particularly not now.' He tapped the letter. 'A most interesting missive arrived by the first post.' He paused, his keen eyes on me. 'Would you care to read it?'

I smiled. 'You know I would.'

Holmes gave me the letter, and sat in the armchair, fingers steepled, to await my verdict. I read aloud:

Cromer House, Nether Walsingham, Norfolk

Dear Mr Holmes,

Please forgive my writing to you like this, but I do not know who else to turn to.

My uncle, Tobias Harding, whom I serve as a companion, died a few days ago. He had always promised me that he would make sure I was provided for after his passing, since I have no closer family of my own. However, when the will was read, he left his whole estate to his younger brother (another uncle of mine), from whom he was estranged. The exception, which has been left to me, is a carved ebony cabinet which stood in his bedroom, and its contents.

I looked up at Holmes, who was watching me. 'Go on,' he said, his eyes gleaming.

The cabinet is a sort of puzzle cabinet. It has many drawers and cubbyholes, and also a secret compartment, which my uncle showed me the trick of. When I learnt of my inheritance, I went straight to the cabinet, examining every drawer. They were all empty. But when I opened the secret compartment I found an envelope, addressed to me in my uncle's writing, containing a single sheet of paper. On the paper, also written by my uncle, was a short poem. I think it is a sort of riddle, but if so, it is beyond my understanding.

The matter is made more urgent because my other uncle, Frank Harding, is arriving soon to take possession of the house and its contents, and I shall have to find another home, as will the cabinet.

Please reply by return if you can help me.

Yours sincerely,

Amelia Harding

'The wire is sent,' said Holmes, springing out of the chair. 'My bag is packed. A train to Norfolk leaves within the hour. The only question, Watson, is whether you will join me.' He paused, his hand on the doorknob.

I thought the matter over for approximately two seconds. 'A short holiday might do me good,' I observed.

'Excellent.' Holmes flung the door open and clattered downstairs. 'Don't wait up, Mrs Hudson,' he called. 'Dr Watson and I are going to Norfolk, and we may be some time.'

II

The trap rattled along the uneven, winding road, jolting us over potholes and stones alike. When we arrived at Fakenham station the town was busy; but the further we travelled, the quieter the road became, till at last I wondered if we would meet another vehicle or horseman before we reached our destination.

Norfolk was no cooler than London; the still air clung to us, as the leaves clung to the trees, defying autumn. There was not a hint of breeze, and the afternoon sun beat down on us until I wriggled in discomfort. Holmes, however, looked as cool as ever; he seemed to have his own internal thermostat, and he sat composed in his town clothes, swaying gently with the motion of the trap.

At last the carriage slowed, and turned a sharp corner at a large copse of trees, and I sensed from the driver's more sedate pace that our destination was close. I was right; for in another quarter-mile a high wall of yellowing stone loomed over us. The carriage rolled between the gate-posts, which were topped with grotesque, intricately-carved beasts, and down the gravel drive.

'Ere y'are,' called the cabman. 'This is Hardings.'

'I thought it was called Cromer House,' I said.

'It may be,' said the cabman, tugging the reins, 'but it's Hardings round here, and always has been.'

I surveyed the house which was growing before us; a rambling edifice built of the same yellowing stone, with arched windows and a cavernous porch which resembled a gaping mouth. A turret stood at each end, with narrow, slitted windows. I swallowed, hard, and looked at Holmes, who seemed impervious to any chilling effect the building might have.

We disembarked with our small luggage, entered the dark porch, and rang the bell. The door opened almost immediately, revealing a slender, fair young woman of middle height dressed in black. 'Mr Holmes?' she asked, turning towards me.

'I am Dr Watson,' I said, smiling. 'This is Mr Holmes.'

'Oh of course, how silly of me.' She bit her lip, and a slight flush came to her pale cheeks. 'I am Amelia Harding.' Her hot, dry hand rested in mine for a moment, and my professional judgement questioned whether she might have a fever. 'Do come in. Would you like some refreshment?'

'Perhaps later,' said Holmes. 'I think our first task, if you do not mind, is to inspect the curious cabinet which you mentioned in your letter, and to see if we can decipher your uncle's poem.'

Miss Harding's large, pale blue eyes rested on Holmes. 'Yes, of course you are right. I will take you to Uncle's bedroom, where the cabinet stands.'

I had been so busy studying Miss Harding that I had barely taken in the interior of the house. Now I looked around me, and saw a dim hall hung with dark paintings, its ceiling so high that the coat stand and few chairs were dwarfed by comparison, like dolls'-house furniture placed in a full-sized dwelling. 'If you would follow me, gentlemen,' murmured Miss Harding, and led the way towards a wide flight of stairs whose mahogany balustrade writhed with vines and leaves beneath the smooth patina of the rail. One flight, two flights, up the shallow steps, until we stood in front of a porticoed door. Miss Harding reached for the brass knob, and twisted.

I do not think I have ever seen so much crammed into a room, before or since. There were glimpses of red silk wallpaper at the cornicing and in occasional gaps, but otherwise the room was lined with bookshelves and cupboards. Small tables stood piled with glass domes and leather-bound volumes and smoking paraphernalia. A winding path led to the four-poster bed, draped in heavy red velvet, and beside it stood a wing-backed leather armchair. The curtains were open, but any light which ventured in seemed to be trapped by the hangings and the shelves and even between the pages of the books, and subdued by the musty, close atmosphere.

'Uncle spent most of his time here,' said Miss Harding. 'When he became more frail, he didn't venture out at all. This room, for the last few months, was his whole world.' I looked about me, and tried to hide my shivering at the thought of an existence ended in this dark, cramped place.

Holmes's eyebrows were raised as he took in his surroundings. 'Which cabinet did your uncle leave to you, Miss Harding? There are quite a few to choose from.'

Miss Harding edged her way into the room, and we followed cautiously. She stopped in front of an ebony cabinet, perhaps five feet tall, its two large doors carved in the pattern of a maze. Its twisted legs ended in clawed feet, and the heads of what appeared to be goblins leered from its top; a rogues' gallery of evil-wishers. 'This is the one.' She opened the double doors to reveal several smaller doors and drawers. 'I put Uncle's letter back in the secret compartment, for safekeeping.'

Miss Harding reached up and opened a drawer near the top of the cabinet, pulling it all the way out. She reached into the space where the drawer had been, and seemed to press something, whereupon another drawer popped out, in which lay a white envelope. She took it, and handed it to Holmes. I was close enough to see the words *To Amelia* penned in wavering script.

Holmes began to pull out the enclosure, then paused. 'May I?' he asked, turning to Miss Harding.

She smiled, a sudden merry smile which lit up her blue eyes even in that dark room. 'But of course,' she said. 'It is what you have come for.'

Holmes mused for a moment, then nodded to himself and drew the sheet of paper from the envelope. 'Come, Watson, let us look together.'

I moved closer, and read the lines written in the same spidery hand:

> *Trapped am I within this bed,*
> *Cabin'd, cribb'd, confined,*
> *Till the world without this room*
> *Barely springs to mind.*
>
> *In the garden zephyrs blow,*
> *I feel them not one bit.*
> *Now my life is bare, austere,*
> *And I tire of it.*
>
> *Take direction while you may,*
> *Draw it to your heart.*
> *Show depression you shall not;*
> *One day we must part.*
>
> *Read my words, and mark my words.*
> *For, when I am gone,*
> *They may hold the key to much;*
> *Words to live upon.*

'Well,' I said, 'I am as puzzled by that as you are, Miss Harding.' She replied with a sweet smile, and we both turned to Holmes. 'Holmes, what do you make of it?'

Was it my imagination, or did a flicker of doubt cross the great detective's face? He tapped the paper. 'I am not sure that it would win any literary prizes,' he said. 'But I have a few ideas that I would like to test.' I waited for him to cross to the cabinet and begin pulling out drawers and trying knobs. But no. He stood gazing at the sheet of paper. 'How long did you serve as companion to your uncle, Miss Harding?' he asked.

'For a year and a half, more or less, s —, Mr Holmes.' Her cheeks flushed a little.

'What sort of man was he? What was his temperament?'

Miss Harding seemed to be considering how to continue. 'You must remember that he was not well. He was nervous, and sometimes irritable. He could not bear the heavy feet and loud voices of some of the servants, and he forbade them from coming upstairs, on pain of instant dismissal.'

'And he was estranged from his brother,' I remarked.

'Quite so, quite so,' mused Holmes. 'Was his

death . . . expected, Miss Harding?'

'I wouldn't say expected,' she said, her blue eyes open wide. 'He had been confined to his room for several months, and the doctor had said that he did not forecast any improvement in my uncle's health, but —' She paused, as if nerving herself for the next part. 'It was still a terrible shock when I came in with his morning tea and — and —'

'Of course.' I moved to Miss Harding's side and led her gently to the armchair. 'I am so sorry.' I cast a reproachful glance at Holmes, who stood unmoved, observing Miss Harding.

'Did you usually bring your uncle his morning tea, Miss Harding?' he asked.

'I did,' she said, her hands twisting. 'He said Anne, the housemaid, was too noisy.'

'What about his valet?'

'He — he had no valet. He said no-one could replace his former man, who had died on the way back from South America.' Miss Harding swallowed. 'Anne looked after his clothes, and he dressed himself, always.'

'Mm,' said Holmes.

The silence lengthened, until the sound of the door-bell made us start. It was followed by banging. We heard feet patter to the door, and a creak, followed by a loud voice. 'About time! What, you think I have all day to stand in the porch waiting for your convenience?'

All the colour had drained from Miss Harding's face. 'That will be my uncle,' she said, in a voice as dry as autumn leaves. 'That will be Mr Frank Harding.'

III

We followed Miss Harding downstairs to find a broad, dark-haired man of about fifty pacing the hallway. He caught sight of Miss Harding, and stopped. 'This is a pretty pass,' he said, offering his hand. 'You must be Amelia.'

'Yes, Amelia Harding,' she said quietly, bending in a curtsey.

'No need for that, you're not a servant,' he said abruptly, and she jerked upright. 'Sorry, sorry,' he said, releasing her hand and stepping back. 'It's been — well — rather a business.' He frowned at Holmes and me, standing at the foot of the stairs. 'Who are these two?'

Holmes advanced, hand outstretched. 'Sherlock Holmes, consulting detective. This is Dr Watson.'

'Charmed, I'm sure,' he said drily. 'I'm Frank Harding. And you are here because…?'

'Miss Harding invited us to try and decipher a

letter which your brother left to her, in the ebony cabinet which she has inherited,' said Holmes smoothly.

'A letter?' His frown deepened as he saw the sheet of paper in Holmes's hand. 'What sort of letter?'

Miss Harding bit her lip, and studied the floor.

'It is a riddle,' said Holmes. 'Miss Harding, may I show it to your uncle?'

She nodded, her eyes still downcast.

Mr Harding held the letter at arm's length and inspected it briefly, then snorted. 'Just the sort of senseless ramble I would have expected from Toby,' he said, returning it. 'He was always odd, but after he came back from South America he was cracked, quite cracked.'

'When was that?' asked Holmes. His voice and manner were casual, to an uninformed observer, but I sensed rather than saw the tension in his frame.

'Seven or eight years ago. Caught some kind of yellow fever while he was out there. I came to see him, when I was allowed, and he was a husk of a man. Rambling about this and that, and eyeing me as if I was going to steal his pocket-watch.' Mr Harding sighed. 'He looked like a ruined house.'

He surveyed the bare, cavernous hall. 'And here I am, saddled with the damn thing, and not a penny to run it.'

'Really?' Holmes raised an eyebrow.

'Yes, really.' A rueful smile transformed Frank Harding's stern face. 'I don't know what Toby spent the family money on, but spend it he did. Old Fosbury wrote me with the details, and once I'd deciphered the lawyer-speak, it turns out that Toby had two hundred pounds in the bank and an empty safe-deposit box. I'd suspect him of hiding his fortune under the floorboards to spite me, but I doubt he had the strength.'

Miss Harding frowned, as if in pain. 'What was he doing in South America, Mr Harding?' I asked, to divert the conversation.

'Damned if I know,' said Frank Harding. 'A crackpot scheme, probably, or looking for more blessed curios to stuff his house with.' He glanced at Miss Harding, and lowered his voice. 'What you must understand is that Toby and I weren't close. He lived here all his life, while I went into the Navy, and then decided that the prospecting of the Merchant Navy was more to my taste. I made my pile, and retired.' I could imagine Frank Harding barking orders on a swaying ship. He caught my look and shrugged. 'Perhaps he grew envious of my exploits, who knows? Him growing dustier and dustier in this junk-shop, while I roamed the world.'

'How long was he away for?' asked Holmes.

'Two years, I think. It's hard to say. He didn't write. I heard of his return through the family doctor.' Frank Harding sighed heavily. 'It isn't a pleasant thought that my only brother was such a curmudgeon, but he was. He just wanted to be left alone, like one of those molluscs that retreats into its shell at the first sign of trouble.'

Holmes turned to Miss Harding. 'Would you agree?' he asked.

Miss Harding looked taken aback. 'I wouldn't have put it quite in that way, Mr Holmes. But yes, my uncle did like his own company. I sometimes —' She paused, as if to work out what she meant, then continued. 'I sometimes felt as if I was there not as a companion, but merely to carry out the tasks which he wasn't strong enough to accomplish.'

'And to bear his bad temper, no doubt,' Frank Harding interjected.

Miss Harding blushed, and fidgeted.

'So.' Frank Harding turned to Holmes. 'Any

luck with the riddle?'

'I believe I am making progress, yes,' said Holmes. 'But I want to talk to a few more people who had dealings with Mr Harding. The family doctor, for instance.'

'You'll be lucky,' said Frank Harding. 'Old Dr Jennings died, what, five years ago, and he was at death's door for a few years before that.'

'I see,' said Holmes. 'Who is — was — Mr Harding's current physician?'

'Dr Bunyan,' said Miss Harding. 'I could send a servant to his practice asking him to call, if you wish?'

'That is a kind offer,' said Holmes. 'However, I think fresh air would do Dr Watson and me good. Does Dr Bunyan live far off?'

'No, his house is a mile away, just before the next village,' said Miss Harding. 'If you turn left out of the gate, it is a pleasant walk. Or James could drive you, if you would find that too far —'

'I think we shall walk, thank you, Miss Harding.' Holmes's eyes settled on her. 'In your estimation, is Dr Bunyan a good doctor?'

'I, um, I couldn't say, for I am very healthy myself,' stammered Miss Harding.

'I see,' said Holmes, with a gleam in his eye.

'Will you be back for dinner?' she asked. 'We usually eat at seven.'

'That would be excellent,' said Holmes.

'Indeed it would,' said Frank Harding. 'Amelia, you can give me a tour of the house while these gentlemen are, er, pursuing their enquiries.' He gave me a sharp look. 'I may as well know what state the place has got itself into.'

'Will you keep it?' asked Holmes.

'Of course I'll keep it!' he snapped. 'There have always been Hardings at Cromer House, and I'm not selling the family home because my idiot of a brother has let it go to rack and ruin.' He stalked away to examine one of the portraits, but the stiffness of his posture betrayed his mood.

'I won't keep you any longer, Miss Harding,' said Holmes, walking towards the door. She followed, and slid back the great bolts which secured the door, but I had already seen the pain which she strove to hide flit across her face.

***

I waited until we were beyond the gates and out of earshot before rounding on Holmes. 'Did you have to cross-examine that poor woman? I thought we were here to solve a riddle, not to probe Miss Harding on her uncle's nature, the propriety of her

140

position, and her opinion of the family doctor!'

Holmes strode on without answering for a few seconds. 'Did you think my questions unfair, then, Watson?'

'I did, yes. Miss Harding was clearly embarrassed and unnerved by your questioning.'

'Good.' We emerged from the shade of trees into full sun, and I blinked. 'I suppose you also disapprove of my question to Frank Harding.'

'About keeping the house? I most certainly do, Holmes. It's none of your business.'

'Mmm.' He strode on. I had difficulty keeping up with him in the blistering heat. 'But you are partial, Watson.'

'I beg your pardon?'

'I have seen how you observe Miss Harding, how you react to her glances, her blushes, her gestures…'

'She is a friendless young woman in an impossible position. I am merely sympathetic to her plight,' I said, with as much dignity as I could muster at the pace we were going. 'Anyway, Holmes…' I paused to catch my breath, then moved in for the kill. 'Are you sure you aren't asking all these questions to hide the fact that you can't unravel the secret of the cabinet?'

'Oh, that,' said Holmes, dismissively. 'No, I am pretty sure that I could turn back now and find the cabinet's secret enclosure in less than five minutes.'

I stopped dead. 'So why are we sweltering in this heat, Holmes?' I demanded.

Holmes seemed as cool as ever as he regarded me. 'Because I have a feeling, and have had it ever since I received Miss Harding's letter, that the secret of the cabinet is only the beginning.' He turned and resumed his march, and I had no choice but to follow.

IV

'What was your opinion of Tobias Harding's state of health, Dr Bunyan?'

The doctor, a plump, sleek man of perhaps thirty, sat back in his chair and considered Holmes's question. 'He wasn't a well man, certainly. I don't think he ever recovered fully from the fever which I understand he caught in South America eight years ago. Although I suspect it was epidemic jaundice.'

'But…' prompted Holmes.

The doctor looked surprised, then smiled. 'You are correct. There is a but. Mr Harding's heartbeat was strong and steady, his limbs were not wasted, he had no digestive complaint that I am aware of; indeed, no ailments at all, beyond a lack of muscle tone. Yet he kept himself shut in that dark room, without even the fresh air from the window, and demanded the blandest of food. It was as if he

143

wanted to be an invalid.'

I shook my head. 'Sometimes our patients are their own worst enemies.'

Dr Bunyan nodded enthusiastically. 'Every time I visited I told him to walk in the garden, build himself up with beef, and live a little. But when I returned, I always found him the same; pale, thin and listless. Poor Miss Harding didn't know what to do for the best, torn between following my advice and obeying her uncle.' He attempted a fierce expression which softened immediately into a faraway look.

'How is Miss Harding's health, doctor? Do you attend her too?' asked Holmes, with the hint of a smile.

Dr Bunyan almost snapped to attention. 'I do not attend Miss Harding as such, but she has been affected by confinement in that room. Miss Harding is paler than she was, and more nervous. I have prescribed her a tonic, but what she needs is rest and a change of scene.'

'Indeed,' said Holmes. 'May I ask . . . were you surprised at the news of Mr Harding's death?'

Dr Bunyan thought, frowning as he traced and retraced a line on the blotter with his finger. 'On one hand, no. He seemed determined to be as ill as he could. But on the other hand, there was no particular reason for him to pass away when he did.'

'And did it appear to be a peaceful death?' I asked.

'Yes. Yes it did. Mr Harding appeared to have died in his sleep.' Dr Bunyan frowned. 'There were no signs of distress, or of anything untoward, if that is what you were thinking. I would certainly have raised the alarm if there were.'

'What did you write on the death certificate?'

'Natural causes,' said the doctor.

'I take it you examined him?' I asked.

'Of course I examined him!' cried Dr Bunyan, half-rising from his chair. 'What are you trying to say?'

'No, no,' I soothed. 'I did not mean any slight on your professionalism. I just wondered if you noticed anything.'

Dr Bunyan relaxed visibly, and sat back down. 'I'll be honest with you gentlemen; I did not linger over the examination. The room was dark as ever, even in morning light, and I did not wish to distress Miss Harding any further. I made sure that Mr Harding's heart had stopped beating, and that there was no hope of revival — which there wasn't, since he must have been dead for at least two hours. His limbs were beginning to stiffen. I checked him for any obvious cause of death, found nothing, and left it at that.'

'So nothing curious at all,' said Holmes.

Dr Bunyan grinned shyly. 'There was one thing… When I lifted the sleeve of Mr Harding's nightshirt to check for a pulse, he had a tattoo of a dragon rising from the waves on his right forearm.' He pointed to the place on his own arm. 'Maybe he got it in South America.'

'How odd,' said Holmes. 'You'd never noticed it before?'

'I never had. Then again, Mr Harding was always dressed when I saw him.'

'I don't suppose you could sketch the tattoo for me?' Holmes took a small notebook and a pen from his pocket, and the doctor pursed his lips as he drew.

'There,' he said. 'That's how I remember it.'

'Very interesting,' said Holmes. 'People can surprise you, can't they?'

'They certainly can.' Dr Bunyan grinned. 'I would never have suspected Mr Harding of having a tattoo. He seemed the sort of man who would never take an unnecessary risk.'

'Quite,' said Holmes.

***

'Holmes, do you suspect —'

'I suspect everyone,' said Holmes, grim-faced and hurrying. 'No, that is not precisely true. I have more than one person in mind, and I cannot say more at present. There is one more call I wish to make before we return to Cromer House and address the cabinet.'

'Where are we going now?' I asked,

'Into the village. You look thirsty, Watson, and I propose a pint of the landlord's finest.' He stopped in the road, loosened his tie, unbuttoned his waistcoat, and assumed a somewhat warm and rumpled appearance. 'Watson, you will do as you are.'

The Five Bells inn was cool and dark. A few drinkers stood at one end of the bar, engaging in banter with the white-haired landlord. He caught my eye as we approached. 'What'll it be, gentlemen?'

'Two pints of your best, if you would,' said Holmes, removing his hat and wiping his forehead with a handkerchief. 'Warm weather, isn't it?'

'It certainly is,' said the landlord. 'And where do you hail from?'

'We're down from London, doing a bit of surveying at Hardings.'

'Hardings, eh? Now that was a business.' He clicked his tongue. 'Poor Miss Harding, cooped up all day with the master and only allowed out to buy food. I'd see her walking by with her little basket, not that I'd expect her to come in here but she always wished me good day.'

General agreement rumbled around the bar like benevolent thunder.

'Did you see much of Mr Harding? I believe he kept himself to himself.'

The man laughed. 'He did! Now Mr Frank I knew well, till he went for a seaman. He'd be in regular, not that his father knew. But Mr Tobias was never a drinker. He came in a few times with his brother as a young man, and he'd sit and make faces over a pint in the corner then leave without so much as a thank-you.' He huffed. 'But you can't choose your lord and master, can you?'

One of the drinkers, a weather-beaten man who looked as if he had seen better days, snorted. 'No, you can't choose your lord and master, and I should know. I'd served the Hardings man and boy, and not been paid too much for it neither. But when Mr Tobias came back from his pleasure trip to America, I was out on my ear as soon as he was out of his bed, because I was too noisy for his delicate ears.'

His lip curled. 'He didn't even have the courage to tell me himself, he got the footman to do it. And while he gave me a character, what use is that when the whole village knows you've been dismissed?' He exhaled heavily. 'Give us another,' he muttered, sliding his glass towards the landlord.

'Right you are, Sam.' The landlord took the glass and bent to the pump. 'I'm just glad he never tried to shut us down,' he said.

'Indeed. A village needs its inn,' said Holmes, taking a deep draught of his ale.

'Well said, sir, and I'd say you need that pint.'

'That I do,' said Holmes. 'But back to work for us now. Come along Watson, you're taking all day.'

'Found anything interesting at the old pile?' asked one of our fellow-drinkers, as I downed the rest of my drink.

'It's a bit precarious,' said Holmes, rising. 'But I expect you knew that already.'

V

The heat of the day was finally beginning to abate as we returned to Cromer House. Holmes's pace had slowed; he strolled, his brow furrowed in thought. He pulled out his pipe, then stowed it in his pocket again. 'There is no time,' he muttered.

'Then why aren't we hurrying, Holmes?'

He shook his head. 'There are many enquiries I would like to make, to be sure; but while a wire is quick, the response may be slow. We must strike now, or lose the opportunity, and yet —' His thoughts turned inward, and I saw that he would divulge nothing until we had reached the house.

This time the housemaid opened the door. 'Miss Harding is in the garden with Mr F — Mr Harding,' she said. 'Shall I inform her that you have returned, sir?' She looked ill at ease, as if she expected to be shouted at.

'Yes please,' said Holmes. 'But just one thing

before you go.' The housemaid hovered, fiddling with the hem of her apron. 'How long have you been a servant here, Anne? It is Anne, isn't it?'

'It is, sir.' She considered. 'Four years, sir.'

'Has any servant worked here for longer than you?'

'James has been here six, I think. There's only Maisie the cook besides me now, and she's served two years.' She moved a little closer. 'The master wasn't an easy man to work for, and the house is so quiet that servants tend not to stay long.'

'I see,' said Holmes. 'When you say that he was not easy to work for —'

'I don't want to talk out of turn,' said the housemaid, wagging her head. 'But it was like walking on eggshells. The slightest thing would upset him. If I made too much noise moving the furniture when I dusted, or dropped a spoon, even, I'd hear about it. I think it was his nerves, but even so —' She came to a sudden halt, and reddened. 'It doesn't sound much, when I say it, but — it hasn't been a pleasant house.'

'Thank you, Anne.'

The housemaid bobbed her head, and tripped away. Holmes watched her go, and I wondered whether he was doing so to avoid meeting my eye.

I was burning to know whether he thought the same as I did. Could it be…? I drifted into a brown study of conjecture and half-thoughts, until I was roused by approaching footsteps. I saw Miss Harding hurrying down the hall, followed by Frank Harding at a marginally more sedate pace.

'Mr Holmes!' she exclaimed, coming to a halt before him and gazing into his face. 'How have your enquiries gone this afternoon?' I felt distinctly relegated, and tried not to be jealous.

'Dr Watson and I have passed a most interesting afternoon,' said Holmes. 'Have you had your tour of the house?' he asked, turning to Mr Harding.

'I have,' said Frank Harding, standing with his hands clasped behind his back. 'It is not as bad as I feared. I was expecting the worst, and for once I have been pleasantly surprised.' He cast a keen look at the pair of us. 'Have you solved the riddle, if riddle it be?'

'I believe so,' said Holmes. 'I am quite happy to test my theory shortly. But first I should like to ask two more things.'

'Fire away,' said Mr Harding.

'The first is rather odd,' said Holmes. 'Would you happen to know if your brother Tobias had a tattoo?'

'Toby?' Frank Harding threw his head back and laughed, then took off his jacket and removed his cufflink, pushing up the sleeve to show a small rope and anchor motif inked just above his wrist. 'He caught sight of this one day when I was on leave, and said it was disgusting. "I can't believe you would voluntarily mutilate yourself," he said, in his mincing voice. So no, if he had a tattoo I would be very surprised.' He resettled his sleeve. 'Why do you ask?'

Holmes and I exchanged glances. 'My next question is for Miss Harding,' said Holmes. 'How did you come to be Mr Harding's companion? Did he engage you, or did you contact him?'

'I wrote to him,' said Miss Harding, her eyes downcast.

'Where were you living at the time?'

'In Norwich. I had been working as a companion to an elderly lady, who had sadly died, and knowing that my uncle lived at the family home, I decided to write and see if I could be useful to him.'

'I see.' Holmes paused. 'And of course you could supply references?'

'Well, no, not from my previous employer,

since she had died —'

'But from the one before that?'

'I — I had no previous employer,' said Miss Harding. 'I had been with Miss Smith for some years.'

'Yet despite your service no-one could supply a reference,' mused Holmes. 'Very well. You said in your letter, Miss Harding, that you had no closer family than your uncle. I assume that therefore you are an orphan.'

Miss Harding nodded, her mouth pressed closed.

'With no brothers and sisters?'

'That is correct,' she said. 'I have no brothers or sisters living.'

'Mr Harding, does that sound right to you?'

Frank Harding raised his eyebrows. 'Certainly my sister Jane and her husband are dead,' he said. 'You must remember that I have spent much of my life at sea, and Jane was the baby of the family. I do seem to remember that Jane mentioned an Amelia in her letters, but I was never a good correspondent.'

'Never mind, Mr Harding,' said Holmes. 'I am sure that Miss Harding can produce papers, or at least *something* which can prove her identity.'

Miss Harding's mouth trembled. Her gaze wavered between Holmes and myself, and finally moved to Frank Harding. Then it dropped to the floor, and her shoulders shook as she struggled to compose herself.

'Can you?' asked Frank Harding, a curious expression on his face.

Miss Harding put her hands over her face as if to hide herself. 'I admit it,' she muttered. 'I am not Amelia Harding.'

'Well!' Frank Harding whistled. 'Who are you, then?' He held out a large handkerchief to Miss Harding, who took it and wiped her eyes. Eventually she was calm enough to speak.

'My name is Hannah Makepeace. I had been asked to leave my post as a governess in Norwich because of — a misunderstanding, and I knew that I would be leaving without a character. I had heard of Mr Harding, shut up in his big house all alone, and I made careful enquiries about his family. When I found out that there was a niece called Amelia, who had fair hair and was roughly my age, I wrote to him in her name.' She swallowed. 'I was desperate, you see. My mistress made sure my name was a byword among her acquaintance, and possibly beyond.'

'And what was this misunderstanding?' Holmes asked.

'It — involved her husband.'

'I see. And Mr Harding engaged you as a companion.'

'It wasn't like that, not at all!' She appeared genuinely horrified, while Frank Harding seemed rather amused. 'I thought that being a relative would keep me from another misunderstanding!' Her gaze moved between us again; but this time her eyes showed anger, not fear. 'You don't know, how could you? The servants at my last place hated me because they thought I gave myself airs, while *he* looked at me as if he had a right to me, just because I was under his roof! I tried to keep out of his way, but he wouldn't have it. And of course when my mistress caught him, I was the one to blame...' Her fists clenched tight. 'What would you have done, in my position?'

'Do you know, Watson,' said Holmes reflectively. 'I think it is time to proceed to the cabinet. Miss — Makepeace, if you would lead the way.'

We ascended to the cramped, airless bedroom and stood before the carved ebony cabinet, which looked no less sinister in the slanting beams of the late-afternoon sun. Holmes pulled out the sheet of paper and consulted it.

'Here is my interpretation,' he said. 'I shall leave the first stanza until later, when it will be more relevant. *In the garden zephyrs blow...*' You are a seafarer, Mr Harding. Which wind is the zephyr?'

'The west wind,' said Mr Harding. 'But what has that got to do with anything?'

'We shall see,' said Holmes, tapping the paper. 'Now, this word *austere*. A perfectly good word, but also not dissimilar from the word auster, which is —'

'The south wind!' exclaimed Frank Harding. 'And this relates to the cabinet?'

'I believe so,' said Holmes. '*Take direction while you may...*'

'So the west, and the south...' Miss Makepeace moved towards the cabinet and began pulling out drawers and opening compartments.

'No!' said Frank Harding. 'It is the other way. A southerly wind blows north, and a westerly blows to the east.' His eyes creased in the manner of a seafarer looking for land, and gleamed as if he had found it. 'Besides, Miss Makepeace,' he added, stepping forward, 'this cabinet was left to

Amelia Harding. You have no claim on it.' He tried to take her arm, but she shook him off, glaring.

'If you would both move back, we shall get to the truth of the matter more quickly,' said Holmes. Both frowned, but did as they were asked.

'Now,' he said, closing the drawers and compartments. 'As Mr Harding says, it is the other way about. A west wind blows towards the east, and a south wind blows towards the north. So if we *take direction,* and open the drawer at the northeast corner of the cabinet —'

'There is nothing,' snapped Miss Makepeace. 'Do you think I haven't had every drawer out a hundred times?'

'I shall *draw it to my heart,*' said Holmes, reading. He gave me the sheet, then reached for the drawer and pulled it from the cabinet, examining it closely and running his fingers over the joints. 'This seems innocent enough. But we have not finished with this remarkable poem.' I gave back the paper. '*Show depression you shall not,*' he muttered, putting his hand into the hole left by the drawer. 'Wait.' He pulled out his handkerchief and wrapped it around his hand. 'It is scant protection, but better than nothing.' He paused. 'If depression is pressing down, perhaps I should try *up*.' He ran his hand along the top of the space and I saw a slight upward motion, followed by a muffled crash as a shallow box fell into view. Within was another white envelope, inscribed in the writing we had come to know. '*To the finder*,' read Holmes.

'Bravo, Holmes!' I cried. 'Come on, open it!'

'Yes, open it!' Frank Harding echoed. 'What was it, "*Words to live upon*"?'

'Indeed,' said Holmes. 'Watson, would you mind putting yourself between the rest of us and the door?'

I raised my eyebrows, but did as he asked.

'What the devil is that for?' Frank Harding scowled.

'A precaution,' said Holmes. 'Mr Harding, given Miss Makepeace's recent revelation, I take it that you can prove your identity, if asked?'

'Of course I can!' Mr Harding snorted. 'I can produce a hundred people ready to swear to it, and a passport and papers.'

'It is as well to make sure,' said Holmes. 'Identity is a slippery thing, especially when it traps you unexpectedly.' He inserted his finger below the seal, ripped the envelope open, and withdrew a long letter accompanied by a further envelope. 'I shall read the letter before opening this enclosure, and see if my suspicion is correct. And Watson, who has been party to my findings, may not be too far behind me.'

He smoothed the letter, and read.

VI

Dear reader,

Well done on your discovery! If I were wearing a hat, I would take it off to you.

But of course I am wearing no hat; for if you are reading this I am dead, and I have a few words to say before I close.

I hope you enjoyed my little poem. I am no poet, but the composition of my puzzle in verse whiled away an hour or so, and I have many of those to spare, confined as I am. Yet I may have fewer than I realise; and this is the matter that concerns me.

Amelia, if you are the finder of this missive, congratulations. You have played a good game, and played to win. Therefore you deserve fortune, since it favours the brave.

However, I suspect that you, gentle reader, are not Amelia. I made this puzzle deliberately obscure in the hope that she would require assistance. If I had intended to leave the estate to Amelia, I would have done so directly. As you will see, I have reasons.

First of all, if you have worked out my puzzle, I suspect that you will also have worked out some of the truth about me. I am not Tobias Harding.

Miss Makepeace gasped, and Frank Harding swore under his breath. Holmes glanced at me, smiled and continued.

My name is Samuel Keen. Or rather it was, for it is so long since anyone addressed me as such that I barely believe it myself. I met Tobias Harding on board the Argus, *returning from Venezuela to England. And it may or may not surprise you, but I was an able seaman.*

'The winds!' exclaimed Frank Harding.

Mr Harding was no sailor. He stayed in his cabin mostly, attended by his man, and the cook thought it was a fine joke to send me with his meals. 'You're peas in a pod!' he would laugh. We were similar in height and colouring, it is true, and had regular features, but Mr Harding was fastidious in his appearance and wore fine clothing, while I was shaggy and dressed in a uniform with more patches than original material. He complained at being on a trade ship — not that he had much choice, since with the trouble brewing in Venezuela he was lucky to get a berth at all. Mr Harding looked at me as if I were a savage, and indeed I suppose I was. I could read and write, more or less, and add a column of figures, and there my formal education had ended.

'But he doesn't write like —' I burst out.

Holmes quelled me with a raised hand, and continued.

You can probably guess the sequel. Mr Harding's nausea and shivering turned out to be not just seasickness, but the beginnings of a fever, which he must have brought aboard with him. He was moved to the sick bay, and his man and I, since we had had repeated contact with him, were put in there too to sink or swim. The sawbones visited daily, but otherwise we were alone, and meals were left outside the door for us.

His man, Miskin, was first to succumb. He had

continued to wait on Mr Harding, and the strain led to his rapid decline. He rallied for a day or two, then turned yellow as parchment. Mr Harding was too ill to pay much attention, but when Miskin breathed his last, I banged at the door and screamed for help. They bundled him in a shroud, and I suspect that he went over the side with little ceremony.

I began to shake and sweat, and I could not tell if my malady was real or brought on by my imagination. Mr Harding was improved; but I had seen how the disease had gone with Miskin.

I am not sure when I had the notion. I think it came upon me gradually. I asked Mr Harding about his life, and what he would do when he returned home. He barely acknowledged me at first; but with nothing else to do he began to respond, boasting of his collections and his valuables and his fine house. And yes, his prized ebony cabinet and the secrets it held. I stored away all I could in my mind; the sound of his voice, his turn of phrase, and of course any information I could obtain of his habits, his home, and his family. We were on reasonably good terms, and I would perform small services for him, as far as I was able. The only exception was *that I would not shave him. My excuse, to my eternal shame, was that I wore a beard, and was out of practice with a razor. Soon he had a ragged beard, too.*

Mr Harding's rally was longer than Miskin's, but not long enough. He went downhill rapidly; and I sensed that the sickness had hold of me as well. I was hot, then cold, and the thought of food made me nauseous. I had to act quickly.

While I had some strength left, I dragged Mr Harding out of bed and across the floor, and hefted him into my cot. I sincerely hope he was too delirious to know what I was about. I took him out of his fine nightshirt, and changed it for my coarse linen. I put the nightshirt on, and with the aid of a pair of scissors and the reflection of my face in the porthole, I trimmed my beard as best I could, and got into Mr Harding's bed.

Mr Harding's end came quickly. I did nothing to hasten it; let me say that now. I would have sat beside him; but I was too feverish to move. I heard his death-rattle, and I was powerless to raise the alarm.

The next thing I remember is being shaken gently by Carter, the sawbones. 'We think you're over the worst, Mr Harding,' he said. I struggled upright, and blessed my good fortune; or I did until I looked in the glass. My yellow flesh hung off me, and my eyes were sunk deep in my face. But we were close to England now; we were approaching my fortune.

My original intention, as much as I had one, was to live quietly till I got my strength back, then realise my capital and go on another voyage from which I would slip into the sort of life I wanted abroad. I spent the rest of this voyage in Mr Harding's cabin, going through his possessions, learning all I could about him. He had kept a journal, and I continued it, imitating his handwriting and his style. I gathered from it that he was a solitary man, and this delighted me. It would make my impersonation easier to sustain.

When I came to Cromer House I lived very quietly, and decreased the risk of detection by dismissing several servants for minor misdemeanours. I always gave them a character, of course. I also quarrelled with Mr Frank Harding, my supposed brother, which grieved me. He was a man whose company, under other circumstances, would have pleased me much. But it was too much of a risk.

I kept to my room mostly, and asked for books

and treasures to be brought to me there, so that I could (re)familiarise myself with them. I read essays, and poetry, and The Times; *I puzzled over Shakespeare, and learned to love him. More and more I found my pleasure not in planning my escape, but in enjoying Mr Harding's possessions, and my original intention to flee was defeated by a strengthening urge to cling to what I had gained. I dared not visit the inn, since I had learnt that Mr Harding was temperate, and I feared meeting a former acquaintance of his who might expose me. The village was out of bounds for the same reason. Sometimes James would take me for a drive, but the trap jolted my now old bones. I used to walk in the garden, but my illness had wasted my muscles and I found even moderate exertion an effort. Me, who had worked a ship for years! I had, I realised, truly become an invalid. I felt as if I had become Tobias Harding, to the point where I wonder if my former life was nothing but a dream.*

Years passed and I buried myself in learning, until I flatter myself that I probably knew as much about Mr Harding's possessions as he had done. But increasingly there were things I wished to do, such as arrange the purchase of new curiosities, which I found hard to accomplish without help.

Yet who could I ask? The servants would not do. I did not want to engage a smart young secretary, for I feared that he would winkle out my secret and hold me to ransom, if not worse.

Miss Harding's letter was a godsend. I replied, and a gentle, meek, attractive young woman of reasonable but not excessive intelligence presented herself. We got on as well as I allowed myself to get on with anyone. And yet as time advanced I began to suspect her; she rarely spoke of family, and when I pressed her, she was evasive. She had brought no references, no credentials, and I believed she was no more a Harding than I. I observed her carefully, and noted her manner towards the doctor, and his towards her. How I longed for an ally; yet I had made sure as part of my deception that I had none!

My suspicion, and I hope I am wrong, is that the pair of them are in league to make away with me. I request bland food to make sure I can detect any strong-tasting poison which might be added. I watch them, and I have seen bottles of 'tonic' pass between them, along with meaningful looks. I know I am growing weaker; but I cannot tell if it is through approaching old age, the deterioration of my condition, or malevolent intent. Hence this letter, which I hope will lead to the discovery of the truth. I have re-made my — Tobias Harding's will, and as part of it I have instructed that my body be interred in a specific location within the family vault. Depending on what you find, I empower you to do with the enclosed envelope and its contents as you see fit.

Yours faithfully,
Samuel Keen/Tobias Harding

Holmes finished reading, and the silence which followed lengthened until it seemed that none of us would ever speak again. It was Miss Harding who broke it. 'I didn't poison him,' she said, her words seeming to come with difficulty. 'I did nothing.' I glanced at Mr Frank Harding, but he was lost in his own thoughts, and I looked away abashed.

Both raised their heads at the sound of ripping paper as Holmes opened the second envelope. 'Share certificates,' he said, flicking through the contents. 'Promissory notes. If these are all valid, the total is around fifteen thousand pounds.'

Frank Harding whistled. 'And what do you plan to do with the enclosure, Mr Holmes?' His voice was casual, but his eyes gleamed.

Holmes crossed the room and rang the bell, and the housemaid appeared at a speed which made me wonder if she had been listening outside. 'I take it the house does not have a telephone?' Holmes asked.

She shook her head, eyes wide.

'Is there a police station in the village?'

Again, the shake of the head.

'Very well; I shall telegraph.' Holmes took out his notebook and sat at the bureau. 'One to . . . was your lawyer's name Fosbury?'

Frank Harding nodded.

'One to a doctor I know in the area, asking him to perform a post-mortem examination.'

Miss Makepeace swallowed, but did not speak.

'And one to the head of the Norfolk Constabulary, inviting a senior officer to pay a visit at his earliest convenience, accompanied by a few men.'

'You can't keep us here,' said Miss Makepeace; but her voice shook.

'I can and I will,' said Holmes. 'There is more than enough to make me suspicious; and until there is proof either way, or I have handed this case to the police, here you will stay.' He tore the sheets out of his notebook and handed them to the housemaid. 'Get James to send these directly.' She bobbed, and backed out of the room. 'And now, we wait.'

'I don't know how I didn't see it,' remarked Frank Harding, shaking his head. 'May I sit?'

'You may,' said Holmes. 'Watson, check him for a gun first, please.' He took a pistol from his own pocket and covered me while I patted Mr Harding down. 'Just a precaution, you understand.'

'Nothing there,' I called.

Frank Harding sank into the nearest chair, and sighed. 'This isn't quite the inheritance I had in mind,' he said.

'No,' said Holmes. 'I doubt it was what Samuel Keen planned, either.'

VII

We set off for London the next morning, after a vigil into the night followed by a lengthy session with the Chief Constable and a pair of detectives. Mr Harding and Miss Makepeace were required to remain in the house for questioning, while we repaired to the inn and enjoyed a hearty meal and what would have been a sound night's sleep if my dreams had not been punctuated with visions of tossing and turning in a fever, while the world rocked around me. I awoke sweating and clammy, the bright sun burning my eyes, and it took me a few moments to come to myself. I staggered to the washstand and peered into the foxed looking-glass, to be sure I really was John Watson.

We caught a mid-morning train, with the purpose of securing a compartment to ourselves, and succeeded in our objective. The train crawled into motion, and I tried to think only of London and the familiar, and put our strange adventure and that sinister house behind us. But it was no good. 'What made you decide to wait before opening the cabinet?' I asked Holmes, eventually, as the train sped through the flat landscape.

Holmes did not answer immediately, but regarded the fields whizzing by outside. 'Why would a sick man set a test for his companion?' he asked. 'That is either a sign of extreme sadism, or a sign that all may not be well. There were too many warning signs; they piled upon each other, and with every one, things grew more convoluted.' He paused. 'I was almost distracted from Miss Harding's history by the suspicion that Tobias Harding was a fraud.' Holmes laughed, but without humour. 'Between them the pair have created a legal conundrum, and I would not care to have the task of unravelling it.'

'Do you think the tattoo Dr Bunyan drew is real?' I asked.

Holmes pursed his lips. 'I imagine so. Dr Bunyan does not seem like a man with the knowledge or the imagination to invent a Japanese *irezumi*. That is what he sketched, and it is plausible that Samuel Keen picked up a tattoo or two on his travels.' He reached for his notebook and showed me Dr Bunyan's drawing. 'It is a point in his favour. I do not actually think he is an accessory to murder, however partial to Miss — Makepeace — he is.'

I shuddered. 'Please don't, Holmes.'

He laughed. 'A sore point, eh, Watson?' I frowned at him, and he subsided immediately. 'I am sorry. She is an attractive woman, to those who like that particular type.'

I grimaced. 'Do you think she had a hand in Keen's death?'

Holmes considered. 'My belief, and I hope that the post-mortem proves me right, is that Samuel Keen killed himself. Not by violence, or an act of self-harm,' he added, as he saw my expression. 'He was so determined not to be found out in his deception that he confined himself to a dry, barren life which, ultimately, was unsustainable. "Cabin'd, cribb'd, confined."' He eyed me. 'Do you recognise the quote, Watson?'

I mused. 'Shakespeare?'

'Yes, from *Macbeth*. "Cabin'd, cribb'd, confined by saucy doubts and fears." Samuel Keen thought he could get away with replacing Tobias Harding as the master of Cromer House, but he lived in constant fear that someone would expose him as an impostor. He forced himself to become Tobias Harding, a suspicious, acquisitive, solitary man. And in that sense, it was Tobias Harding, the man he sought to replace, who killed Samuel Keen.' His voice was low, his face serious. 'At any rate, it is out of our hands now.' He gazed out of the window again, and I watched his still profile as the lowering, darkening cloud gave way, and the first heavy drops of blessed rain thudded against the glass.

A One Pipe Problem

'A walk, perhaps.'

Sherlock Holmes's gaze shifted from the syringe-case on the mantelpiece until his eyes rested incuriously on me. 'Stop trying to divert me, Watson.'

'A walk would do you good,' I persisted. 'Certainly more good than —'

'That is a matter of opinion,' said Holmes, raising himself to a sitting position on the sofa. 'I am sure you mean well, Watson, but your prescription of fresh air and exercise is no more than a sticking-plaster over the real problem — the sad lack of stimulation which London affords my brain at the present time.'

'And the whole world outside this stuffy, smoky room is insufficient for your brain, I suppose,' I said, with rather bad grace.

Holmes smiled. 'I apologise, Watson. I know I am not a good patient. But I did not ask you to prescribe for me.' His gaze returned to the syringe-case.

'I challenge you.'

Holmes's brow furrowed for a moment; then an expression of amused resignation spread over his countenance. 'You . . . challenge me?'

'I do.' I rose from the armchair and collected the *Times* from the floor, where Holmes had flung it after a careless perusal on its arrival. I dropped it into Holmes's lap. 'How many times have you said that all the intrigue in London lurks within the pages of a newspaper, Holmes?'

Holmes laid a long, thin hand on the paper. 'I may have made the observation once or twice, but I hardly think —'

'Then prove it.' I tried to keep the exasperation out of my voice. 'You are a scientist by nature and by training, Holmes. Make your proof.' I sat back down, rather more heavily than I had meant.

Holmes's eyes rested on me again, and his face was inscrutable. 'You are out of temper, Watson,' he observed. 'But very well. I shall humour your fancy, and perhaps it will bear fruit. Perhaps I shall find a one-pipe problem within these flimsy sheets.' He sighed, leaned against the sofa-cushions, and opened the newspaper.

For some time there was no noise but the gentle rustle of pages, and the ticking of the mantel clock

— and with every tick I knew that the chance of Holmes finding something of interest within the *Times* was running out. I imagined his eyes scanning the columns of print, hunting for a hare to start, a fox to be run to earth. As the clock ticked on I visualised his pace slowing, his attention wandering, until he would let the paper fall, and go to the mantelpiece, and fetch —

'Hmm.'

I almost sat bolt upright, and gripped the arms of my chair to stop myself. I waited for the sound of a turning page, but it did not come.

'*Hmm.*'

'What is it, Holmes?' I burst out.

The paper lowered to reveal a changed Holmes. His eyes were bright, his expression alert. 'At the bottom of page seven, Watson.'

I rose and came over, and he tapped the paper at the foot of the last column.

A MOST PARTICULAR THIEF

Police were called to a robbery at a chandler's shop in Poplar on Tuesday to find that the perpetrator had very specific requirements.

During the robbery, which took place overnight, the only items taken were a whole drum of best-quality rope and a large iron hook. The takings in the till were untouched, along with several other valuable items.

Proprietors of businesses are reminded to be vigilant, secure their premises, and deposit takings in a safe or at their bank, to reduce temptation. The shop owner, William Baxter, knew nothing of the crime until he came down from his quarters above the shop the next morning.

'What a strange occurrence,' I remarked.

'Yes,' said Holmes. He smiled as he gently laid the newspaper down, still open. 'A seemingly bungled robbery where the only things taken are heavy, bulky, and of comparatively low value, and the takings are left in the till.' He paused. 'Rope, and a hook. Rope — a whole drum of best quality rope — and a large iron hook…' His voice sank to a whisper, and his eyes gleamed. '*Enough rope to hang yourself.*'

***

Holmes scribbled a note and rang the bell. 'Run this to the telegraph office for me, Billy,' he said, giving the page half a crown.

'Do I wait for an answer, sir?' Billy asked.

'I think not,' said Holmes. 'If Lestrade is out on

a case he may not answer for some time.' He flung himself onto the sofa, then got up again. 'It would be as well to be ready,' he said, and disappeared into his bedroom. 'Ring for hot water, would you, Watson?' he called.

I smiled, and pulled the bell.

Fifteen minutes later Holmes emerged from his room, freshly shaved and dressed with his characteristic neatness. 'Ready to face the world,' he said, smiling. 'Perhaps we should make our way to Poplar.'

The back door creaked. 'Unless I am much mistaken, Billy has returned,' Holmes said softly. He remained standing, listening, and presently we heard the page's light steps pattering up the stairs.

'There must be an answer,' I breathed.

A tap at the door, and Billy entered, a little out of breath.

'The clerk called me back, sir, just as I was leaving,' he said. 'I ran all the way.'

He took a slip of paper from his pocket and passed it to Holmes, who read it and frowned. 'That will be all, Billy,' he said. He held out the paper to me.

I read the terse reply: *A practical joke not a police matter Lestrade.*

I looked up. 'Do you think he's right?'

Holmes shook his head. 'Lestrade is like an underground train; if a matter is off his track, it is of no concern to him. A theft of rope and a hook is hardly serious, in itself. But I would dearly like to know what steps have been taken. I am tempted to bypass Lestrade altogether, and go to Poplar on my own account...' He smiled at my disapproving expression. 'But I shall not. I shall be polite, and face the lion in his lair.'

'Scotland Yard?'

'Scotland Yard.'

***

'Nonsense,' Inspector Lestrade said decisively from behind his desk.

'Really, Inspector?' asked Holmes.

Inspector Lestrade made a noise which somehow combined a snort and a pshaw. 'Really, Mr Holmes. As far as I am concerned it *is* nonsense, and a thorough waste of police time. One of my best officers dragged out to Poplar, to interview a shopkeeper who saw nothing, heard nothing, and lost precious little.'

'Did he take a statement?' asked Holmes.

The inspector looked at him levelly. 'Why are you interested?'

'I think there's something behind this,' said Holmes. He leaned down, his hands flat on the desk. 'Can I see the report?'

The inspector's chair scraped back with a suddenness that made me start. He stalked across to a filing cabinet in the corner, muttering, and extracted a single sheet from the front of the top drawer. 'There,' he said, laying it on the desk. 'It will take you less than a minute to read, and then you'll know as much of the matter as anyone. I hope it satisfies you.'

I read over Holmes's shoulder.

William Baxter, 52, lives alone over the shop. He retired at a quarter past ten on the night of the event in question, and slept soundly until half past five in the morning, when he came downstairs and found the shop door open. On checking through the shop inventory, he found that the following two items were missing: a drum of rope, and a large iron hook, around two feet long. No money had been taken.

Mr Baxter heard no disturbance during the night. He does not know of anyone who might want to play a prank on him, or do him harm.

On examining the door of the shop, the lock

had been picked. No force appears to have been used to gain entry. I advised Mr Baxter to engage a locksmith, and in the meantime to fit a bolt to the door. I am not convinced he will take my advice. He seemed puzzled, rather than frightened.

'And there you have it,' said Lestrade. 'Perhaps the thief will return and make off with a box of ship's biscuit, or some lamp oil.' He whisked the paper from the desk and replaced it in the cabinet, closing the drawer with an air of finality.

'I might go and visit Mr Baxter,' said Holmes.

The inspector resumed his seat. 'You do that, Mr Holmes. You go to Poplar and see if you can get the man his rope and hook back. In the meantime, I have important cases to attend to.' He drew a stack of files towards him, and I gathered our interview was at an end.

***

My heart sank as the cab pulled up outside a dingy shop at the end of a mean little street. The board above the door said *Chandler*, in faded blue paint, and someone had added *Baxter* in much smaller, uneven black letters beneath.

'This is it, then,' I said. 'All the way out here,

for this.' How I regretted my challenge to Holmes . . . but what else could I have done?

Holmes himself, however, seemed buoyant in mood. He jumped down and paid the driver, then led the way to the shop door, whistling.

A cracked bell rang as he pushed the door open. The shop was dark and gloomy, and it took my eyes a while to adjust. When they did, I saw a large round-shouldered man, wearing a dirty apron, standing behind the shop counter.

'Mr Baxter?' asked Holmes, venturing further in.

'Aye,' said the man, warily. His voice was deep and slow.

'My name is Sherlock Holmes, and I am a detective. I have come to talk to you about the robbery which took place here a few nights ago.'

'I put a bolt on, like the p'liceman said.' Baxter shuffled towards us and pointed to a smallish bolt affixed halfway up the door. 'Ain't been no more trouble.'

'Good, good.' Holmes followed him towards the counter. 'How long have you had this shop?'

'Ten year, maybe eleven,' Mr Baxter said, indifferently. 'It were my uncle's shop, an' as he had daughters, it passed to me. Worked here all my life, just about, so it were only right.'

'Of course. And does it do well?'

A sort of bark popped out of Mr Baxter. 'I'm still 'ere, ain't I.'

'And you're sure the only things taken in the break-in were some rope and a hook?'

Baxter sucked his teeth. 'Only things I saw were gone.' He waved an arm at his sawdust-smelling stock, piled in boxes and barrels and trays. 'I ain't gonna count every nail now, am I?'

'Of course not,' soothed Holmes. 'And you can't think of anyone with a grudge against you? Or who might play a joke on you?'

Mr Baxter thought for a long time before shaking his head. 'I ain't a joking man,' he said, eventually. 'An' most of my customers I've known since I were knee-high to me uncle. I give 'em a good deal, see.'

'I see.' Holmes consulted his watch. 'Well, Dr Watson and I shall leave you for the present. However, we shall return this evening and keep watch in the shop. I have a distinct feeling that something will happen tonight, and I want to be here when it does.'

'But I put a bolt on!' Baxter protested. Then his eyes narrowed. 'How do I know you ain't the robbers, come to finish the job off?'

'Inspector Lestrade can swear to our identity,' said Holmes, giving the man a card, which he peered at and stowed in his apron-pocket. 'We shall return not later than nine o'clock.'

'So long as you don't expect me to sit up with you,' grumbled Baxter. 'If you gents want to listen to me snoring all night, it's your funeral.'

***

'Holmes, do you really think anything is going to happen?'

It was, as far as I could tell, past eleven o'clock at night. I was cold and stiff despite my warm clothes, and the smell in Baxter's shop made me feel faintly nauseous.

I had asked to be dropped off at my practice on the way back from Poplar; I had been neglecting it, and I thought I might as well achieve something in an otherwise wasted day. Holmes had agreed, provided I was at Baker Street for seven o'clock sharp.

'Will you wire Lestrade?' I had asked.

Holmes's mouth tightened in a firm line. 'Lestrade has washed his hands of the matter,' he said. 'I doubt he would help if he could.'

And now, shivering in the dark, damp shop, I

wished I had washed my hands of the matter too.

A sharp creak from upstairs made me jump. 'You still 'ere?' William Baxter called, but his voice had a note of fear in it. He had retired at ten o'clock, and we had heard nothing from him until now.

'We're still here,' Holmes called back. 'What is it?'

'Thought I 'eard a noise.' The stairs creaked and Baxter appeared, still in his clothes. He clutched a tin plate, on which a candle-end flickered feebly. 'A scraping noise, outside the door.' He shuddered. 'I looked out, but I couldn't see nothing.'

'The bolt is drawn,' said Holmes. 'I have checked it. We haven't heard a thing.'

'You sure?' asked Baxter, frowning. He padded to the door. 'I know it's locked, I checked it meself...' Holmes and I watched him feel for the key, on a chain round his neck, then laboriously feel the bolt —

And the next sensation was a soaking pad being pressed over my nose and mouth, and the sweet, familiar smell of chloroform. I was not unconscious; but my arms and legs were heavy and uncoordinated. I felt sure hands grasping me, binding my ankles to the chair I sat on and my hands behind me. Out of the corner of my eye, I saw that the same was happening to Holmes, though he fought valiantly.

'Good evening, gentlemen,' said a cultured voice from the darkness. 'Is all secure?'

The man we knew as Baxter walked across, and ran his hands over first Holmes's, then my bonds. 'It is, sir,' he said, and his voice, while still Cockney, was less rough.

'Excellent. In that case...' A match flared, and was applied to a lantern.

And as the light grew, I saw a face I had not seen for many years. Older, thinner, more lined, but still with that white mark on the forehead.

The face of murderer, thief, smasher and forger John Clay, the fourth smartest man in London.

'Won't you say good evening to me?' He chuckled and held out a hand. 'Oh, but you can't greet me properly at the moment, can you?'

'Watson, I am truly sorry.' Holmes's voice was thick, his words slurred and indistinct.

I said nothing.

'I have prepared a little surprise for you,' said Clay. 'Would you like to see?'

He walked to the centre of the room and lifted

the lantern above his head. In the flickering light I saw two large iron hooks, two dangling ropes, and two hangman's nooses.

***

'Any last requests?' asked John Clay. 'The end, when it comes, will be swift. I've used the best-quality rope, you see.'

'Might I smoke a pipe?' asked Holmes.

John Clay considered. 'I don't see why not,' he said. 'It will give me time to explain myself.' He drew a pipe and a tobacco pouch from his pocket, and Holmes made a face. 'Sorry, but I'm not delving in *your* pockets, Sherlock Holmes. For all I know you've got poison darts or a mousetrap in there.'

'And how I wish I had,' said Holmes.

'Oh, do be quiet,' said Clay, stuffing tobacco into the pipe, lighting it, and putting it into Holmes's mouth. 'Anything for you, Dr Watson?'

I remained silent. I did not trust myself to speak. After all the adventures Holmes and I had had together, this was how it would end; strung up in a chandler's shop in Poplar.

John Clay shrugged. 'Suit yourself,' he said, and drew up a chair, straddling it and resting his elbows on the back. 'I've been waiting to do this for a long time,' he said, grinning. 'After you got me taken up over the small matter of the City and Suburban bank robbery — and such a fine plan it was, too...'

'You should have hung for that,' said Holmes, around his pipe. He didn't sound angry, more matter-of-fact.

'Ah, but I had a good lawyer. The best-quality lawyer, in fact.' I swear John Clay's eyes twinkled.

'Indeed you did,' said Holmes. 'I made a note of his name.'

'And of course I have been a model prisoner,' said John Clay. 'No trouble at all, that's me.'

'What have you done with the real Baxter?' I asked. My mouth felt strange, as if I had borrowed it and wasn't used to it yet. 'Have you killed him?'

Clay shook his head vigorously. 'Noooo. He's bound, gagged and blindfolded in the cellar, and has been since we popped in on Tuesday. Don't worry, he'll be quite all right. Well, if they find him when they find you two, anyway.' He paused. 'I don't suppose you let Inspector Lestrade in on your little mission, did you? No, I didn't think so. I always said your glory-hunting would be the death of you, Holmes, and by God I was right.' He grinned, and in the lantern light his expression resembled a devil's mask. 'I thought I'd have to try harder, Holmes, but you took the bait at my very first attempt.'

'The newspaper,' I murmured.

'Very good, Dr Watson!' John Clay clapped me on the shoulder, and I winced. 'One of my associates is a typesetter at the *Times*, and it was the work of a moment to devise an intriguing little vignette and ask him to slip it in.'

'*Enough rope to hang yourself*,' Holmes murmured, and for the first time I heard bitterness in his voice. 'I should have known.'

'Indeed.' Clay beamed. 'And here we are.'

'Yes,' said Holmes, his voice dull. 'Here we are.'

The door burst off its hinges with a deafening crash. 'Police! Stay where you are!'

Clay's men scrambled towards the rear of the shop, but policemen swarmed through the back entrance, two for every man. John Clay himself stood firm; but his smile had transmuted to something utterly ghastly.

'Good evening, Mr Holmes,' said Inspector Gregson, snapping handcuffs on John Clay's wrists. 'Now then, Mr Clay, it seems like no time at all since our last meeting.'

'Holmes,' I whispered, and my voice was hoarse. 'You knew…'

Holmes spat out John Clay's pipe. 'I must apologise again, Watson. Yes, I knew from the moment I set eyes on that little story in the *Times* that John Clay was behind it. It could have been written for me — and it was, to lure me in. The artistic flourishes — the rope, the hook, the untouched money in the till — those, and the sheer audacity of the crime all pointed to John Clay, deviser of the Red-Headed League, as surely as if he had signed the article. All I had to do was visit Baxter's shop to organise a night-time vigil, make sure the police would be on hand to rescue us, and convince you that I had no back-up planned. For which I apologise a third time; but if you had known Inspector Gregson and his men were outside, Watson, you would never have been so convincing in your despair. And then Mr Clay here might have smelt a rat, even as he gloated over his victory.' The policeman working on Holmes's bonds stepped back, and he stretched his arms and flexed his fingers. 'Ah, that's better, thank you. There's a shopkeeper downstairs who'll need your services, too.'

'Thank you so much for your deception,

Holmes,' I said, a trifle sourly. 'I honestly thought we were going to die.'

'Not this time.' Holmes stood, a little gingerly, and, released in turn from my bonds, I rubbed my sore wrists and ankles. 'Thank you, Watson.'

I raised an eyebrow. 'Excuse me?'

Holmes bent to retrieve John Clay's pipe, and handed it to me. 'For diverting me with a one-pipe problem.' And seeing his expression of quiet triumph made our night of terror almost — almost — seem worthwhile.

ACKNOWLEDGEMENTS

First of all, thank you to everyone who has beta-read and commented on the books in this box set: Ruth Cunliffe, Julie Eger, Paula Harmon, Judith Leask, Stephen Lenhardt, Bobbi Lerman, and Mike Williams.

Thanks as always to John Croall for his meticulous proofreading, howler-catching and general expertise. Any errors which remain are, of course, entirely down to me.

But as ever, the biggest thank-you goes to my husband Stephen Lenhardt — supporter of spooky goings-on.

And finally, thank you for reading! I hope you've enjoyed it, and if you would like to leave a short review on Amazon, Goodreads or elsewhere, I'd really appreciate it.

FONT AND IMAGE CREDITS

Fonts: Selfish by Misprinted Type (freeware): http://www.misprintedtype.com/

Balthazar by Dario Manuel Muhafara: https://fonts.google.com/specimen/Balthazar. Licensed under SIL Open Font License, version 1.1: http://scripts.sil.org/OFL

Graphics:

Cityscape: *On the rooftops of London* in the National Library of Ireland photo stream on flickr: https://www.flickr.com/photos/nlireland/8096307482. No known copyright restrictions, image modified.

Cobbles: *Cobblestone* by obsidianphotography: http://www.pixabay.com (CC0, image modified).

Silhouette: *Man Silhouette Walking* by Mohamed Ibrahim: http://www.clker.com/clipart-70434.html (CC0).

Cover created using GIMP image editor.

ABOUT THE AUTHOR

Liz Hedgecock grew up in London, England, did an English degree, and then took forever to start writing. After several years working in the National Health Service, some short stories crept into the world. A few even won prizes. Then the stories started to grow longer…

Now Liz travels between the nineteenth and twenty-first centuries, murdering people. To be fair, she does usually clean up after herself.

Liz's reimaginings of Sherlock Holmes, her Pippa Parker cozy mystery series, and the Caster & Fleet Victorian mystery series (written with Paula Harmon) are available in ebook and paperback.

Liz lives in Cheshire with her husband and two sons, and when she's not writing or child-wrangling you can usually find her reading, messing about on Twitter, or cooing over stuff in museums and art galleries. That's her story, anyway, and she's sticking to it.

You can also find Liz here:

http://lizhedgecock.wordpress.com/

http://www.facebook.com/lizhedgecockwrites

http://twitter.com/lizhedgecock

https://www.goodreads.com/lizhedgecock

BOOKS BY LIZ HEDGECOCK

Short stories

The Secret Notebook of Sherlock Holmes
Bitesize

Halloween Sherlock series (novelettes)

The Case of the Snow-White Lady
Sherlock Holmes and the Deathly Fog
The Case of the Curious Cabinet

Sherlock & Jack series (novellas)

A Jar Of Thursday
Something Blue
A Phoenix Rises (winter 2018)

Mrs Hudson & Sherlock Holmes series (novels)

A House Of Mirrors
In Sherlock's Shadow (autumn 2018)

Pippa Parker Mysteries (novels)
Murder At The Playgroup
Murder In The Choir
A Fete Worse Than Death
Murder In The Meadow (2018)

Caster & Fleet Mysteries (with Paula Harmon)
The Case of the Black Tulips
The Case of the Runaway Client
The Case of the Deceased Clerk

WHITE
RHINO
BOOKS